MY HOMEWORK ATE MY DOG!

By
Derek Taylor Kent

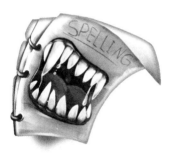

www.WhimsicalWorldBooks.com
www.DerekTaylorKent.com

TABLE
OF
CONTENTS

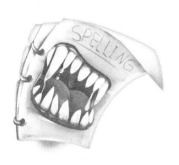

CONTENTS

CHAPTER 1
THE DAY WE MOVED

$\mathbf{T}$he ceiling crashed down in front of me.

The flames had burst out of control in just the few moments it took to pull in the garden hose from the front yard. Now a wall of fire blocked my way out the front door.

There was no way out.

The thickness of the smoke felt like scalding syrup in my throat and burned my eyes even though I was squinting them shut. Then, over the crackling and hissing, I heard Beast barking.

Crawling beneath the river of smoke, I found my best friend cowering in the laundry room dryer. Shaking with fear myself, and with no better plan, I joined my pet beagle in the dryer. I shut the hatch, and watched through the small circular window as my house crumbled.

The fireman said he wouldn't have found us in time if he hadn't heard a faint whisper through the roaring fire telling him to check the laundry room. He pulled me out of the dryer, covered me in a fireproof blanket, and raced toward the back door, carrying me in his arms.

He couldn't hear me screaming that Beast was still in the dryer.

I tried to squirm free, but the fireman clutched me so tight, I had no choice but to curl up and bite his hand. He dropped me with a yelp. I fell on the searing hot floor and ran as fast as I could through the blaze as the fireman chased after me.

1

When I found Beast, I took off the fireproof blanket and wrapped it around him before I was quickly snatched up again. The fireman dashed toward the exit, leaping over fiery beams, holding me tighter than before. I pressed Beast against my chest with all my strength.

With amazing agility, the fireman hurdled through the shattered back door like a tiger jumping through a ring of fire. As I lay sprawled on the street, coughing out the last of the smoke, Beast began licking the soot from my face and eyes. We watched in disbelief as everything the Berkman family owned became nothing more than a heap of ash and rubble.

It felt awful to lose all our stuff—the TVs, the clothes, the computers, the furniture. But the worst part for me was that I lost my entire comic book collection that I spent three years and every dime of my allowance on. All my favorite characters, all my favorite stories, all my favorite artists... They were nothing more than dust in the sky.

And it was my fault.

Beast and I were supposed to be staying next door with our neighbor, Mrs. Atkins. I may have "accidentally" spilled some NyQuil in her afternoon tea and snuck into my house through my bedroom window. You didn't hear that from me though.

Despite warnings about not playing with fire, I decided to play astronauts with Beast. I built a rocketship out of old boxes. We put on our space helmets. I took out a match and lit the ignition — just a collection of napkins and old newspapers stuffed into a thermos. I thought we were safe in our tiled kitchen, but when a draft blew the fiery shreds of paper against the curtains, things got bad fast.

Both my parents were at work while the house was burning. They rushed over when they heard the news. I thought they would be furious, but my mom just hugged me tightly crying, "Rudy! Thank heavens! We heard they couldn't find you!"

I think most kids would remember this day as the day their house burnt down. For me, I remember it as the day my family decided to move to Danville.

Following that incident, I was accepted into Danville Reformatory—a reform school for "challenging" boys and girls that was showing remarkable results. Every angry, rebellious kid who entered Danville Reformatory on the verge of failing out of school was miraculously turned into a perfect, straight-A student.

The man responsible was Dr. Lyman Yux, the mayor of Danville. He had taken control of the school system as his first act once in power.

Being an eleven-year-old kid, the last thing I wanted was to go to reform school in a new city and leave all my friends, but my bad behavior had just burnt down the family house. Not to mention it had nearly killed my best friend. Maybe it was time to change, time to "straighten up and fly right" as my dad suggested.

What was strange was that in my mind, I was a good kid. I never meant to do anything bad. It's just that bad things always seemed to happen that I got blamed for. Like this one time when I was playing wrestling with my friend, Nick. I decided to try a move on Nick called "The Cobra Strike." It looked really cool on TV. Well, unlike what happens on TV, Nick's mouth ended up hitting the edge of my desk and his two front teeth got knocked out. Now he has two fake teeth in their place and he looks like a bunny rabbit. His dentist says he'll grow into them, but after a year I still want to offer him my carrot every lunch time.

Despite the unfortunate incident, Nick was still my best friend. As the days passed and my parents were making all the arrangements for our new life while living in a small motel room on the edge of town, I grew more and more furious that I was not only moving hundreds of miles away from Nick, but also being sent to a school for bad kids.

"Listen, Rudy," Mom told me, "it's not that we think you're a bad kid. It's just that Danville Reformatory is considered the best school in the country right now. They've made a special point of accepting kids with discipline problems to show how their system can turn any kid around. We have to at least give it a chance."

I tried to explain that I would act better. That I would never play with fire again. But it was clear my opinion wasn't going to change anyone's mind.

In less than a week, the car was packed up with the little we had left. The Berkmans were on their way to Danville.

As I waved goodbye to the town of Deep Valley, little did I know I was also waving goodbye to my last days as a normal kid.

CHAPTER 2
THE BEST CITY IN THE WORLD

As we drove into Danville, we passed under an enormous sign that read:

Welcome to Danville. Why ever leave?

I felt like I was walking into Disneyland for the first time. The sun was shining, the streets were sparkling, the birds were singing, and everyone was happy.

Families waved to us from the sidewalk and from inside the stores as we drove down the street. They could tell we were new in town as everything we had left was hitched on top of the small SUV and wrapped in Dad's spare carpets.

The decision to move to Danville was sealed when my dad got a job offer to manage the Carpet Diem that had just opened in Danville. As we were driving along the highway, I was still in a rotten mood and Dad tried to make me feel better. "Rudy," he told me, "I know moving to a new city is tough on a kid. Grandpa Stu was in the military, and I lived in *five* different cities before I was ten."

I thought it was strange that Dad told me that because he rarely mentioned Grandpa Stu. They say Grandpa "went a little crazy" in his old age. He had been in a mental institution as far back as I could remember. I hadn't even seen him since my fourth birthday party, when he grabbed the piñata bat out of my hands and started whacking a poor clown who was making balloon animals. He was sent to the mental hospital soon after that.

Even at the age of four, I was so embarrassed by my Grandpa Stu, I never wanted to see him again. Whenever my friends asked where my Grandpa was on Grandparents Day at school, I always said he was dead. That way, I didn't have to explain where he really was.

Grandpa Stu did give me one thing, for which I am always grateful. At that party on my fourth birthday, I opened a small box from Grandpa. Inside was Beast.

My dad continued, "Now that I'll be the boss at Carpet Diem, you can come by and hang out with me and all those super-cool carpets as much as you want!"

Carpet Diem is a chain of carpet stores my dad works for. The name is a play-on-words of the Latin phrase Carpe Diem, which means "seize the day." Thus, when people hear Carpet Diem, they are supposed to get it in their head that they want to "seize the carpet." Even though literally it just means "carpet day."

Inside the car were me, Dad, Mom, and Beast. I named Beast after my favorite comic book hero—Beast from the X-Men. He was a brilliant doctor that got transformed into a giant, blue gorilla. Things like that seem to happen a lot to scientists in the comic book world. I think that's why I want to become I scientist when I grow up.

Unlike his namesake, Beast is not blue. Like most beagles, he's a bit of brown, a bit of white, and a bit of black—like a s'mores that barks.

We pulled into the driveway of our new house at 706 Cheswick Lane.

"Look at this place, Rudy. The Berkmans have finally made it, eh?" Dad could be a real cornball sometimes, but it was true. The house was huge compared to our one-story house in Deep Valley.

Mom looked even more amazed than me. I don't think she really believed what Dad had been promising us until she actually saw it for herself. As soon as Dad heard I was accepted into Danville Reformatory, he started searching online for new houses in Danville. He made an offer on this one over the phone. The most amazing part was as soon as the realtor heard our house in Deep Valley had burnt down, she cut the price in half if we moved in that week. So except for the few pictures online, this was our first time seeing the house.

"Well," Mom said, "it definitely needs a few rose bushes in front to add some color."

Mom worked as a florist back in Deep Valley. She had to quit her job to move to Danville. Despite jokes my friends like to make, being a florist doesn't mean she builds floors, it means she works in a flower shop. She was excited to finally have a front yard big enough to plant her dream garden.

"So you like it, Abby?" Dad asked, sheepishly.

"It seems very nice, Bernie. Although, I don't see a mailbox anywhere." I could sense her thinking this was too good to be true.

Beast jumped out of the car and started rolling in the grass on the front lawn. I started rolling around with him, but Mom bellowed, "Rudy, you can play tomorrow. Today we have to carry in boxes and start unpacking."

I pretended not to hear her and pulled Beast's favorite tennis ball from my pocket. He jumped on me so quickly that I fell backward and felt something sharp dig into my back. I rolled over and saw a piece of wood with jagged edges sticking up from the ground. I knew exactly what it was.

"Mom! I found the mailbox!"

Mom came over and said, "Oh my. Someone must have hit it with their car. We'll get a new one right away so we can start getting our mail. And no more horsing around, you! Start carrying in boxes!"

Grumbling, I dragged myself over to the car, but before I could even lift the first box, a strange man grabbed my arm and yelled, "Don't you touch that!"

 7

CHAPTER 3
NO DAY IN THE PARK

..."Because we're going to carry all your boxes for ya! I'm your neighbor, Alan Waverly, and this is my wife, Barbara."

Soon after the Waverlys, the Metzgers came, then the Johnsons and the Hansens. The whole neighborhood showed up and did all our moving for us. When the truck arrived with our brand-new furniture, our neighbors carried in the couches, the cabinets, the beds...everything! What we thought would take all day was done in less than an hour with everyone helping.

I asked Mr. Waverly where all the kids in the neighborhood were.

"They're at home studying for the first day of school, of course."

"But school hasn't started yet. How could they already be studying?" I asked.

Mr. Waverly replied, "They got their textbooks last week, so they're getting ahead on their work."

That made no sense to me. For the first time I felt very scared about this new place.

"Don't worry, Rudy. I have a son your age named Bobby. Before he started Danville Reformatory last year, he wouldn't touch his homework either. Now we can't get him to stop! I'll tell him to find you in school on Monday. He'll show you the ropes."

I spent the rest of the afternoon playing with Beast. If Danville Reformatory was so hard a school that the kids would be studying on a beautiful Saturday afternoon before school even started, there wouldn't be much playtime in our future.

*****

The next day I woke up to the feeling of Beast licking my face as soon as the sun came up. It was his usual routine.

I unpacked all my boxes and tried to make my room look like it did back in Deep Valley. I pinned up my new comic book posters, I hung up my new shirts, and I arranged my desk with pencils, pens, and paper. I even had my own bathroom for the first time. I was thrilled to finally have space for my own soap and shampoo without all of Mom and Dad's things clogging up the counter space.

"Sheesh," I thought to myself, "maybe if I burn down this house we can move into a mansion next time." I felt guilty after I thought that.

After a long morning of helping Mom and Dad unpack boxes, I made myself a pb and j sandwich, put it in my backpack, and dashed off with Beast to the park I noticed when we drove into town.

We got to Danville Park and to my surprise, there still weren't any kids to be seen. There were plenty of adults jogging, playing basketball, and having barbecues, but the playground was completely empty.

"Cool," I thought. "No waiting for the swings in this town."

I sat in the sand, pulled out my sandwich and a dog biscuit for Beast. We ate our lunch together in the sand. When we finished, I pulled a frisbee out of my backpack and said to Beast:

"Listen, we're in a new place now, and I'm supposed to change into a new, well-behaved kid. If I have to change, that means you have to change, too."

Beast groaned "Arrrooo" as if he understood what I was saying. I knew he couldn't really understand me, but it always amazed me how he really seemed to be able to.

"I know, I know," I said. "Change is never easy, but maybe it will be good for us. I'm going to teach you a whole new set of tricks. Let's start with one you know. Up!"

At the command of 'up' Beast leaped as high as he could into the air and landed with a big smile. I fed him a small reward treat, which he excitedly gobbled up.

"Okay, now it's time for the new stuff. Look, I brought this frisbee for you. When I throw it, I want you to catch it in your mouth. Got it?"

Beast gave me a look that seemed to say, "Are you kidding me?"

I threw the frisbee across the playground. Beast followed the frisbee with his eyes but didn't move an inch. It landed with a thud on the grass. He looked back at me with a grin and a tail wag as if to say, *Nice throw! I don't know why you did it, but nice throw!*

I walked Beast over to the frisbee. It was time to get serious. I reached into my backpack and pulled out a special doggy treat that looked like a tiny hot dog. Beast got excited and tried to eat it from my hand, but I pulled it away.

"Nuh, uh," I said. "You want this treat, you have to catch the frisbee in your mouth. Like this."

I put the frisbee in my mouth and went "Grrrr!" to show him what he was supposed to do. His eyes widened as if he was thinking, "Have you lost your mind?"

I held up the treat for him to make sure he understood, then threw the frisbee across the park. This time, Beast took off after it.

"Yeah! Go Beast!" I cheered.

Beast was a tad overweight from living the easy life the last few years, but he moved his legs as fast as he could and huffed and puffed after the flying disk. Beast had amazingly caught up with it and made a spectacular leap to catch the frisbee in his mouth.

Unfortunately, Beast was so focused on the frisbee, he didn't the notice the tree right in front of him. CLUNK! He crashed headfirst into the tree trunk and plopped over onto the grass. The frisbee landed softly on the ground in front of him.

When I ran over to him, Beast had already picked himself up. He staggered dizzily, then picked up the frisbee in his mouth, dropped it into my hand and wagged his tail, expecting the treat. I thought about it for a second and decided I didn't want to encourage his clumsiness, so I just gave him half a hot dog.

"Nice try," I said, patting him on the head. Beast snarled as he ate his small reward.

That's when I heard the music.

"Look, Beast! The ice cream man is here!"

The small white truck with colorful pictures of popsicles and ice cream bars pulled up to the curb. Since there were no kids around, I was the only one who wanted any ice cream. Once again, I didn't have to wait in a long line.

The ice cream man popped his head out of the truck. He was thin with long, black hair and a big bushy mustache that had curls on both ends. He looked like someone who had just been fired from the circus.

"Ladies and Gentlemen, step right up and taste the most delicious ice cream in the history of the world!" He even talked like he was just fired from the circus.

"Why, hello there, young Rudy Berkman! What can I get for you?"

"Hey, how did you know my name?" I asked.

11

"Oh, um...well...everyone knows your family moved into town yesterday, and I know absolutely, positively everyone in this town. Using my amazing brain power, I concluded you must be the kid from our town's newest family. It is a pleasure to meet you, sir. The name's Ice Cream Ivan."

"Hi, Ice Cream Ivan. If you don't mind my asking, how do you stay in business when there aren't any kids around to buy your ice cream?

Ice Cream Ivan laughed. "Ladies and Gentlemen, it looks like we have a child prodigy right here in the audience! To be honest, young man, kids haven't gotten any ice cream at all in the last seven years, not since that Lyman Yux became Mayor."

"Why?" I asked.

"Well, I can't say I know for sure. Maybe that's something you can help me figure out."

Ice Cream Ivan's smile dropped. Then he whispered to me under his breath, "Rudy, is anybody looking over here right now?"

I scanned the park. No one seemed to be looking at us.

"No."

"Listen," he whispered intensely. "These folks around here are watching your every move. They're all bad Ankaras."

"Ankaras? What's an Ank-"

"Shhh!! One of them may have super-hearing and could be listening to us. Just heed my advice. There's hardly anybody in this town you can trust, especially the adults. Nothing here is what it seems. Find someone you can trust and watch each other's backs at all times."

Then, as quickly as it disappeared, Ice Cream Ivan's jubilant smile returned. "And for the new kid in town, I hereby present one cherry popsicle free of charge," Ice Cream Ivan exclaimed, handing me the popsicle while making the sound of roaring applause with his mouth.

"My work here is done! You've been a fantastic crowd. I'll see you all next time!"

I turned around and saw there was still nobody within a hundred feet of us. Ivan winked at me, then sped off in his tiny truck.

Something told me I probably shouldn't eat that popsicle. I threw it away in the garbage and ran home with Beast as fast as I could.

That night I decided to go to sleep early. Usually, I would stay up late playing games with my headphones on under the covers, but tomorrow was the first day of school, and I had a feeling I would need to have my wits about me.

CHAPTER 4
THE FIRST DAY OF SCHOOL

Monday morning. The first day of sixth grade.

My digital watch read 7:52 a.m. School started at 8:00 a.m., but the halls were empty.

I stepped into room 4-B. Uh oh.

The first thing I noticed was that every boy was wearing gray shorts, a white-collared shirt, black dress shoes, and a red tie. The girls looked the same except with a gray dress.

There I was. Ripped blue jeans, old sneakers, X-Men T-shirt. Not good.

There was only one desk open in the middle of the room. I was eight minutes early, but apparently I was the last one to arrive.

All the boys' hair was perfectly trimmed without one hair out of place. The girls had matching haircuts with bangs down to the middle of their foreheads. The ends were cropped evenly above their shoulders.

I personally gave up on my hair a long time ago. It curls as tight as stretched ribbon and fros out into a perfect woolly dome no matter what I do. The one good thing about my puffy hair is that it creates the illusion that I'm about three inches taller. That works out well seeing as I'm about two inches shorter than most boys my age.

I sat down and introduced myself to a neatly-combed blonde kid sitting next to me. "Hi, I'm—

"Rudy Berkman. I know. I'm Bobby Waverly. I saved that seat for you."

"Thanks. Wait, you're my neighbor!"

"Yes. My father told me to look out for you. And I have done so."

Strange kid.

"Hey," I whispered, "I didn't know this school had a uniform."

"It doesn't. This is how we like to dress."

I laughed. Loud.

"What's so funny?" Bobby asked, completely serious.

"You're kidding, right? No kid would wear a tie because he wants to."

"I do. We all do. Right?"

Together, the whole class said, "Yes, Bobby."

This was creepy. I noticed everyone was sitting straight up in their desks with their hands folded. Not one student was talking, chattering, giggling, eating glue, or... doing anything!

"Don't worry," said Bobby, "soon you'll be like us."

Be like them? That's the last thing in the world I wanted. I may be a smart kid (maybe a little too smart for my own good), but I'm still a kid. I felt like I was surrounded by a bunch of tiny adults. For the first time, I felt very lonely. I missed my old school and my old friends more than I could say.

15

I wondered what my friends were doing in their classroom right now in Deep Valley. Heck, I even missed Brett Looger.

I couldn't believe I had that thought right after it passed through my head. Brett Looger had once broken my skateboard in half after I made the mistake of accidentally splashing him when I skated through a puddle. And that was one of our more friendly encounters.

The morning bell rang and the teacher burst through the classroom door huffing and puffing as if he had just ran a race. He was a small, nervous-looking man. His head was almost completely bald with wisps of gray hair on the sides and crooked glasses on the end of his nose.

He carried an old satchel and a tin lunchbox. His eyes twitched and darted around as if were being followed by someone with ill intent. He set his satchel and lunchbox on the desk, then wrote his name on the board.

"Hello, my name is Mr. T-Thompson," he said with a slight tremble in his voice. "Before we start our f-f-first lesson, I have to ask if any of you have s-s-seen...have you seen..."

Mr. Thompson abruptly stopped speaking, although his mouth kept moving. Then, a trail of red mist began seeping into the room from underneath the door. The mist slithered across the floor like a million red ants. Then it shot upward, straight into Mr. Thompson's mouth!

Mr. Thompson erupted into a terrible coughing fit. He lunged toward his tin lunchbox. Opening it as fast as he could, he pulled out a vial of green liquid. He chugged it down, only to spit it all out moments later like a broken sprinkler.

None of the kids looked scared or even the slightest bit worried.

After a few seconds, he collapsed silent and motionless on the floor, pools of green and red mist seeping from his mouth.

CHAPTER 5
MS. COVENLY

I was frozen in shock. Since none of the kids seemed to be reacting, I jumped out of my seat and ran for help. Before I could even reach the door, it flung open and two men wearing white coats and red ties stepped inside.

"We're doctors," they said, matter-of-factly. "Remain calm and stay in your seats."

I sat back down in my chair and tried to stop my legs from shaking. As the doctors pulled Mr. Thompson out into the hallway, a startling vision strolled into the room that almost made me completely forget about what had just happened.

She had long, wavy brown hair, tanned skin, and was possibly the tallest woman I'd ever seen. She looked like she might have been a professional basketball player, or maybe even a beach volleyball player like the ones on ESPN3. Not that I ever watch that.

She wore a tight white blouse and gray skirt that looked constrictive, but I wasn't going to say anything. She looked at me sharply and I felt a rush of dizziness. Could this be the most beautiful woman in the world?

"Hello, class! It seems Mr. Thompson has taken ill. But it doesn't really matter because he was fired last year and still tried to show up for work today. Pathetic. I am your real teacher. My name is Ms. Covenly."

I noticed she was carrying a huge stack of papers. They went from her waist all the way past her head! Was this our work? My palms started sweating.

Ms. Covenly erased Mr. Thompson's name and wrote her name on the blackboard. She took a handful of papers from the very top of her huge stack and said:

"Since it's your first day, I think it's the perfect time for your first pop quiz!"

She suddenly became much uglier to me. I groaned, but the class started cheering! They shouted together, "Hooray!" and then were quiet. I raised my hand as she started handing out the quizzes.

"Yes?"

"Ms. Covenly, how can we have a pop quiz when we haven't learned anything yet?"

The class laughed in unison, "Ha. Ha." Then hushed quickly.

"Well, you've had your textbooks for a week. I assume you started self-learning them already?"

Self-learning? "No, I'm new. I didn't know that..."

"Ah yes, you're Rudy Berkman. The little fire-starter. Didn't you get your advance homework assignment in the mail?"

"In the mail? No, our mailbox was broken off when we moved in. We haven't gotten any mail yet."

"No mailbox? Hm. That's strange. Well, just try your best. I'm sure you'll do fine."

I agreed and started to do the quiz. There were numbers in the math section I didn't even recognize. Words in the definitions section I couldn't even pronounce. I trudged through the quiz on the verge of tears, knowing I was certain to get an F.

18

The rest of the class blazed through the quiz, smiling the whole time. Bobby finished first and shouted, "Done!"

The class put down their pencils and cheered, "Bobby, Bobby, Bobby!" then hushed, picked up their pencils, and resumed working.

I looked up at Ms. Covenly, hoping she would see my anguished expression and take pity. Ms. Covenly didn't look at me, though. She never even raised her eyes to check for cheating. Her nose was buried in a magazine called The Danville Dandy.

Then, ever so casually, she reached into her purse and pulled out...

A mouse!

She held it up by its tail as it squirmed and squealed. I looked around the room to get the class's attention but no one would look up from their quiz. All I could do was sit there aghast as Ms. Covenly carefully dangled the mouse in the air...and dropped it in her mouth.

She took a few hard bites, slurped up the tail, then swallowed it with one loud gulp.

I started screaming.

CHAPTER 6
THINGS GET WORSE

The whole class turned and looked at me.

Ms. Covenly inquired with concern, "What's the matter, Rudy?"

"WHAT'S THE MATTER?? You ate a mouse! Didn't you all see that? She took a mouse out of her purse and ate it!"

The class looked at Ms. Covenly then laughed at me. In her hand she held a green apple with a bite taken out of it.

"Now you listen to me, Rudy Berkman. I will have no more disruptions in my class. One more outburst and you can go show Principal Pooly how funny you think you are."

"But, but I—

"Not another word. Class, please forget you heard that and finish your quiz."

The kids' faces immediately went blank, as if they really did forget everything they had just heard. They turned their attention back to the quiz, but I kept my head up and saw the apple in Ms. Covenly's hand transform into a vile-looking rat.

I kept my mouth shut. Ms. Covenly smiled at me warmly as her teeth turned into sharp fangs and she devoured the hideous rodent. I nearly threw up, but I decided to figure out later if something was seriously wrong here or if I was going crazy.

After an hour, everyone turned in their quizzes, but mine was virtually blank. I couldn't understand a word on it. The lunch bell couldn't have come any sooner.

*****

Lunch was a very strict procedure. The class walked in a straight line from the classroom to the lunch hall. One by one we were given trays that were filled up with five scoops of slop and gruel that were completely unrecognizable to me.

During lunch I was determined to meet a regular kid like me, but I couldn't find one. Everyone was wearing the choice white shirts and red ties and acting more like robots than kids.

I sat down next to Bobby at the class lunch table.

"What is this stuff?" I asked him.

"It's lunch," he said.

"I know that, but what is it?"

"I'm not sure. I just know I like it."

The lunch lady, Mrs. Krimbly, blew on a whistle and everyone started eating. I laughed to myself when I heard that her name was *Mrs.* Krimbly. She had the face of a vulture with wild, frizzy, red hair and even had a huge, red pimple oozing between her eyes. Well, I guess there's a lid for every pot as they say.

Everyone was eating, chewing, and taking sips of their drinks in unison. I decided to try going along with it and took a small bite of the grey stuff on my left. I immediately spit it out. It was the most horrible thing I'd ever tasted. It tasted like a mixture of charcoal, vinegar, and grass.

Gathering my courage, I tried the yellow stuff on my right. That made me throw up in my mouth. It was horseradish, liver, and rotten fish heads.

Mrs. Krimbly came from behind me and said in a harsh, hawkish voice, "What's the matter? Not to your liking?"

I replied as nicely as possible, "This isn't quite what I'm used to. Do you have a peanut butter and jelly sandwich somewhere?"

She started laughing. Her disgusting, fishy breath almost made me pass out. "Ha Ha Ha! Nothing like that! You just don't like it because it's healthy. You keep eating it. Soon you won't be able to get enough of it."

I nodded and tried one more bite of the purple stuff. After that, I lost my appetite anyway.

*****

The rest of the day in class, Ms. Covenly lectured on various subjects. The problem was she talked so fast, I didn't have time to write everything down in my notebook. I felt like I was missing more than half of what she was saying. When I asked her to repeat something, she told me to just copy a classmate's notes later.

At the end of the day, she gave us our homework assignment to read and answer questions from the textbooks. The final bell rang. As we were walking out, she told me to stay after class, which I agreed to hesitantly.

"Rudy," she said smiling, "I noticed you had quite a bit of trouble with the quiz today. Are you proud of starting your first day at Danville Reformatory with an F?"

"No, I told you I didn't know..."

"No excuses, Rudy Berkman. Your parents sent you here to make you an A student, and that's just what I plan to make you. I've put together this special homework assignment for you. I promise that once you finish it, things will change for the best."

Ms. Covenly pulled a piece of paper from the middle of her enormous stack, folded it twice and dropped it in my backpack.

"I look forward to a more productive day from you tomorrow. And if you finish your homework with all the right answers, I may throw out your score from today's quiz."

I nodded my head and left the classroom. As soon as the door closed behind me, I could have sworn I heard a loud cackle from inside.

CHAPTER 7
PRINCIPAL POOLY

Nothing feels better than those first few minutes of freedom at the end of a school day, knowing that the worst of it is over. Until, of course, you remember that you still have two more hours of grueling homework as soon as you get home.

I walked down the hallway to the pick-up circle when I heard a voice call from behind me.

"Rudy Berkman!"

I turned and saw a large, almost perfectly round man bounding toward me. He was very oily with a big, gummy smile, a red bow tie and thick black glasses. His greasy black hair was combed over his entire scalp. He took hold of both my hands and started shaking them vigorously. His hands were cold and sweaty.

"Rudy Berkman, I'm Principal Pooly. It is a pleasure to meet you!"

"Hi, Principal Pooly. Um, you too."

Mr. Pooly couldn't wipe the stupid grin off his face as he continued to forcefully shake my hands.

"We are very happy to finally have you with us. If there's anything I can do to make your school experience better, just drop in and let me know."

I never even met the principal of my last school, much less have him suck up to me like this. I had no idea why he was doing it, but I decided to seize the opportunity.

"Since you mention it, the food could be better. *Much* better."

"The food? Hmm. Interesting. I'll bring that up with Mrs. Krimbly right away. Thank you!"

At that, he stopped shaking my hands and quickly changed his posture, becoming more authoritative and deepening his voice.

"Now be a good boy and go straight home and do your homework."

He started giggling to himself as if he had done something very naughty. Then he turned around, wiped his brow, and disappeared around the corner. I immediately started wiping his hand-sweat off on my jeans. Gross. However, the more I wiped them off, the wetter my hands felt. I looked down at my hands and passed out on the spot.

They were covered in blood.

CHAPTER 8
THE HORRIBLE HOMEWORK

I opened my eyes to the feeling of a cold, damp cloth on my forehead.

I was back at home in my bed. Beast was snuggled next to me. I scratched him behind his ears, where he likes it the best. He responded by turning his head and licking my hands. That's when I remembered. My mom removed the damp cloth when I opened my eyes.

"Mom, did you see the blood on my hands? Did you clean it off? What happened?"

"Don't sit up too fast. Just take it easy," Mom said, soothingly. "The school nurse found you unconscious in the hallway and called us to come get you."

Dad walked in carrying a big pile of carpet samples. "They said there was a gas leak in the school today. That's what made you faint. Wow, feel how soft this blue carpet is. "

"Gas leak?" I blurted, disbelieving. "But there was blood on my hands! The principal shook my hands and then I saw blood on them and I..."

"No, there was no blood on your hands," Mom said chuckling. "They told us that the gas may have made you think you were seeing strange things. But don't worry, the school is all fixed now and safe for tomorrow."

Was that it? Was that the answer? A gas leak? Did I really imagine all those things I saw today?

Mom continued, "We also met your teacher, Ms. Covenly, while we were there. She told us she's concerned that you're coming in behind the rest of the class."

Dad added, "She also stressed how important it is for you to do this first homework assignment to get you caught up. You let me know if you need any help. I'll be in my office feeling these carpet samples. Feel free to join me! Boy, they're soft."

"Sure, Dad. Thanks." I honestly don't know why he still asks me to feel his carpet samples. I told him I had had enough by the time I was five.

Dad turned back and said, "And Rudy, if you don't mind, take a look around the school and see if any of the rooms need new carpets."

Then there was a knock at the front door. Mom and Dad went downstairs to answer it.

*****

After a delicious dinner in bed of Mom's Shake 'n' Bake chicken legs, I felt strong enough to go to my desk and start my homework.

I pulled out the sheet Ms. Covenly had given me and nearly choked. *Question One: Why are cats better pets than dogs?*

I looked down at Beast asleep at my feet. "Beast, are cats better pets than you?" Beast let out an annoyed growl, then fell back to sleep underneath my desk. "That's right," I said to him.

I wrote angrily on page – *Cats are NOT better pets than dogs because dogs can fetch, go swimming, and they bark when there's danger.*

Question Two: What happens to naughty children who play with fire?

Now I was getting really angry. Ms. Covenly obviously just wanted to embarrass me.

Even more forcefully I wrote: *We get sent to Danville Reformatory and have to answer stupid homework questions.*

I wished someone was there with me to share in the humor, but a sleeping Beast would have to do.

Question Three: Why is your grandfather in an institution for crazy people?

What? How did she know about Grandpa Stu? I didn't care about my quiz score any more. I grabbed the homework paper and crumpled it into a ball. I wasn't going to let anyone ever see that question.

But why did my hands feel wet again? I stared in horror. Blood was seeping from my palms. It oozed onto the ball of crinkled homework paper.

In a panic, I threw the homework into the trash. I ran toward the door, but my chest of drawers slid in front of me, blocking the way out! I tried to push the chest of drawers to the side, but the middle drawer shot out and hit me hard in the stomach. As I tumbled onto the floor, I tried to scream, but the wind was knocked out of me.

The windows shut one by one all by themselves. The lights were flashing on and off. My clothes flew out of the closet and tied themselves around my arms and legs, making it impossible for me to move.

Wrapped up like a cocoon, I rose into the air.

I tried screaming again, but my bandana stuffed itself inside my mouth. My belt tied itself around my face so I couldn't spit the bandana out. Tears of fear poured from my eyes. I could only hope this was a dream.

Floating in mid-air and helplessly bound, I watched with horror as my homework started coming to life.

A bolt of electricity shot out from a power socket. The floating paper started gyrating, jerking, and pulsating with energy.

In seconds the paper grew five times in size. It folded itself into a large terrible mouth with rows of fierce sharp teeth. Bubbling drool spilled onto the floor. It was like staring into the gaping maw of a Tyrannosaurus Rex.

Slowly, I started floating toward the gruesome mouth. I tried with all my strength to free myself, but it was useless. I couldn't scream. The jaws were chomping the air in anticipation and cackling with glee. I was going to be eaten alive.

It was then that a glob of drool from the mouth landed on Beast. And he finally woke up.

Beast had always been a gentle soul. He had never bitten me or any of my friends. But I must say, he truly lived up to his name during the next moments.

Beast quickly realized the situation. He bared his own sharp teeth and started barking and snarling viciously. The hovering jaws turned away from me and looked down at Beast. Streams of slimy drool poured all over Beast, making him even madder.

In a show of athleticism I had never seen from him, Beast leapt onto the chair and flung himself at the mouth, ripping it apart in a furious snapping frenzy. Shreds of paper flew about the room like New Year's confetti. The paper mouth tried to get away, but Beast's jaws were locked onto it with a death grip.

The clothes unwrapped themselves from me, dropping me hard onto the floor. Sweaters and pants surged toward Beast, trying to pull him off of the mouth. Finally they succeeded, but Beast tore off a good chunk of paper with it.

The mouth shrieked in pain and fluttered in the air trying to pull itself together. Just as they had done to me, my clothes were now wrapping themselves around Beast. My belt clamped his snout shut.

I ran to free him, but then my own bed sheets sprang off the bed and ensnared me, leaving me wriggling and helpless on the floor.

The enormous paper mouth again advanced toward me. The sheets lifted me up into the air. They were delivering me toward the hideous mouth like a loaf of bread into an oven.

I thought I was about to be swallowed whole, but then Beast miraculously broke free from the clothes. He vaulted off my bed, and dove straight into the heaving jaws of the mouth.

My cry of "Nooo!" was muffled by Beast's tennis ball suddenly wedging itself between my teeth.

I managed to get one arm free from the sheets and grabbed onto Beast's collar. The mouth jerked back and forth, forcing Beast down its dark gully. I tried desperately to pull out my best friend, but the mouth soon closed around Beast's head. Razor-sharp teeth pierced into my hand. Streams of blood ran down my arm.

Beast let out a soft whimper that seemed to say, "goodbye."

The pain was too much. I let go.

After I'd pulled my hand out, the paper mouth sealed shut. For a few seconds, I saw the outline of Beast struggling inside of it. It looked like when Beast played with me on my bed and I would throw a sheet over him and watch him try to find his way out.

The paper started flattening itself down on Beast like a trash compactor. There was nothing I could do. The mouth was soon a thin sheet of paper again. All signs of Beast were gone.

I could only watch in silent horror as a window opened, the paper folded itself into a glider, and shot out of the room into the distance.

CHAPTER 9
AFTERMATH

After the glider sailed off, everything in my room went back to normal. The clothes flew back into the closet, the chest of drawers moved back into position, the sheets dropped me back into the desk chair. The wound on my hand sealed and the blood disappeared.

On my desk was a note that read: "Dear Mom and Dad, Went out for a walk. Be back soon. – Rudy."

I swung open my bedroom door and ran downstairs.

"Mom! Dad!"

I ran down the stairs so fast I nearly tripped and broke my neck. I found my parents sprawled on the couch, fast asleep.

"MOM! DAD!"

They didn't wake up. I shook them. Nothing. I would have started to panic, but then I heard my dad's signature buzz saw snore. "HRGAGAGAGA....HRRGAGAGAGA..."

On the coffee table in front of them was a box of chocolates. Empty wrappers were strewn about. A note sitting next to it read: From your neighbors...

It was clear to me that things were not right in Danville.

I ran into the front yard. "Beast! BEEEEAST!"

No answer.

I sprinted around the house, darted through the neighbors' yards, then found myself at the edge of the neighborhood where Bellway Forest started. I was out of breath and sucked in air deeply. The chirping of crickets was practically deafening in the eerie darkness.

I heard a howling in the distance. Was that Beast? Or a wolf? Standing there, I became consumed by fear. What was I doing? Beast was gone and I certainly wasn't going to find him all by myself in the middle of the night.

Fear moved my legs even faster back home. Once inside, I thought better of going upstairs. I curled up next to my comatose parents on the couch. I don't remember how, but somehow, I fell asleep.

*****

The sunrise woke me up. I was back in my bed and the blinds were open. It was the first time I could remember Beast not licking my face to wake me up. I trembled with an overwhelming sadness. Maybe everything was a dream. Maybe Beast was downstairs eating his kibble.

I called to Beast, but there was no response. I shuffled to my desk, not wanting to look. But there it was. The note.

"Good morning, Rudy!" My mom stood at the doorway, fully dressed, holding a glass of orange juice. "C'mon! Your breakfast is on the table!"

Something was wrong here. My mom never looked this good or acted so cheerful in the morning. And I'd never seen her out of her bathrobe before I left for school. The smell coming from downstairs was tantalizing. I followed my nose.

I sat at the table with Dad as Mom danced around the kitchen preparing chocolate chip pancakes. Dad couldn't stop staring at Mom with a silly grin on his face. My eyes were still searching for some sign of Beast.

32

Mom turned on the radio so she could listen to an interview with Dr. Lyman Yux, the mayor of Danville. Dr. Yux was going on and on about how his plan for education had made Danville the smartest town in the world. All of its graduates were attending "top ten" colleges and many older graduates were now running the country's largest corporations.

"Isn't he a great man?" waxed my mom. "He really has it all figured out."

There was a dreaminess in her voice and eyes I had never seen before. She gazed through the kitchen window oblivious to everything except Dr. Yux's speech. She never even asked me if I was feeling better. Since she was in another world, I turned to my dad sitting next to me.

"Dad, have you seen Beast today?"

"No, I thought he was upstairs with you."

"Mom, have you seen Beast?"

"Beast? No. He hasn't touched his breakfast."

I was now sure that everything really did happen. I didn't know where or how to begin telling them the horror story. I decided not to for now. Even my kooky dad would never believe me. They'd probably think I was making up an excuse for letting Beast get out.

"Rudy," Dad said, "we told you not to leave your window open. Beast probably crawled out onto the roof, then jumped onto the shed. Now he could be anywhere in the neighborhood."

Mom placed the plate of pancakes in front of us. "Don't worry, honey. I'll look for Beast while you're at school."

"I'll even help during my lunch break," Dad chimed.

I nodded silently. There was only one person who knew where Beast was. She was going to hear from me as soon as I stepped into the classroom.

"Oh, by the way," said Dad, "how did that homework assignment go?"

I choked on my milk.

CHAPTER 10
THE SECOND DAY OF SCHOOL

I walked into the classroom ten minutes early at 7:50 a.m. Ms. Covenly was already at her desk in front of two large towers of papers. She was grading homework while the rest of the class sat quietly with perfect posture and their hands folded.

Ms. Covenly turned from her papers and looked me up and down. I was dressed in the same clothes as yesterday. Something made me not trust my other clothes.

"You didn't do your homework, did you?"

The class gasped.

"Well, I was about to do it," I retorted. "The funny thing is, before I even started, it came to life, ate my dog, and disappeared."

The class laughed abruptly and then was quiet.

"That's very funny," she snorted. "So instead of your dog eating your homework, your homework ate your dog. That's the most creative excuse I've heard in a long—

Her condescending tone made me lose it. With one mighty swing of my right arm, I knocked over one of the towers of papers, shouting, "WHERE'S MY DOG? I KNOW YOU HAVE HIM! YOU BETTER GIVE HIM BACK!"

Papers swirled around me in a whirlwind. My eyes welled with tears and my chest heaved from the emotion of the moment. Ms. Covenly's face became stern. She squinted her eyes at me.

"Mr. Berkman," she hissed, "we do not yell at our teachers at *thisss* school. You just got yourself a week's detention."

"You think I care? I want my dog back!"

I'd gone this far already, so I figured I'd show her how serious I truly was. I jumped onto her desk and punched wildly at the other enormous stack of papers. They also went flying into the air. Then I started kicking all her supplies off the table – the pencils, the pens, the stapler, the paper clips.

I screamed in a terrible tantrum. Papers and supplies littered the floor as if a tornado hit. The class gaped at the unthinkable scene.

Ms. Covenly stood up and glared at me with seething scorn. Her eyes glowed as if there were a fire behind them. As soon as our eyes met, I felt my body go rigid. I fell off the desk into her arms.

I wanted to kick and squirm but my body was stiff as stone. She carried me out of the class all the way to Principal Pooly's office. My body did not return to normal until she set me down in the office chair.

"You are not to come back to class until you're ready to behave like everyone else!" She stormed out, leaving me in front of the very scared-looking secretary.

Then, Principal Pooly, with his red bow tie and greased-back hair, emerged from his office.

With a very disappointed tone, he shook his head and muttered, "Rudy, Rudy, Rudy...let's have a talk."

*****

Principal Pooly's office looked like any other principal's office, except that behind his desk hung a painting of the famous Danville mayor, Dr. Lyman Yux. Dr. Yux's face had a look of vision and determination. His snow-white hair flowed down his shoulders and his long, scary eyebrows stretched outward like hairy white wings. Though it was just a portrait, his piercing gray eyes seemed alive.

Principal Pooly sat in a large red-leather chair while I sat in front of him in one of the plastic classroom variety.

"You like the painting?" he asked.

I looked down and shrugged, frightened and embarrassed to be sitting in front of him.

"It's an original," he continued. "Painted by the best artist in Danville, Lilly Barton. All she paints are portraits of Dr. Lyman Yux. It would have cost a fortune, but she donated it to the school."

"I guess it's nice."

"It's a masterpiece! Almost as great as the man himself. He made this town what it is when he became mayor seven years ago. So, what seems to be the problem, Mr. Berkman?"

I was desperate for someone to believe me. Someone I could trust. I told him the whole story, which he took in with keen interest.

"That's quite a story, Rudy."

"It's the truth," I said.

"Oh, I truly believe that you think it's the truth. But listen to yourself. Don't you think it's possible that you dreamed all these events and your dog just ran away on his own?"

"Then how do you explain *this*?"

I pulled the note out of my backpack and slammed it on his desk.

"I didn't write that," I said with assertion. "I never went for a walk. It just appeared on my desk after the homework flew out the window with my dog."

Principal Pooly leaned back in his chair, looking at the note. He adjusted his thick glasses, took out a cloth and wiped beads of sweat off his brow.

"Rudy, I don't see anything."

"What are you talking about? Look what it says! I didn't write that note. That's not my signature!"

"No...what I mean is..." Principal Pooly removed his glasses, squinted his eyes, and the note burst into flames, vanishing into dust. "I don't see any note."

I was too shocked to respond. I wanted to rush out of the room, but my bottom felt like it was glued to the seat.

"Now, Mr. Berkman," he scowled, lowering his glasses, "instead of making disruptions and fighting against everything, why don't you try going along with things around here? Then things might fall into place and these bad things will stop happening."

"Yes, sir," I nodded, scared that I might be the next thing to burst into flames. I definitely did not have a friend in Principal Pooly.

*****

I spent the rest of the morning writing an apology note to Ms. Covenly and my class, promising I would stop making up stories and causing disruptions. For the second day in a row, the lunch bell couldn't have come any sooner.

I entered the lunch hall late. My class was already sitting down at their table. I asked if they could make room, but Bobby turned around and said sharply, "Sorry, Rudy. Out of space. Find another table." No one from my class would even look at me.

"What about that space right there?" I said, pointing at an empty chair across from Bobby.

"That's for another new kid who came in after you left. He's in the restroom."

I ended up finding a space on the edge of the bench at the 8th grade table. They let me sit there provided I gave them my lunch portions, which I was more than happy to do.

Today I was smart and brought Mom's leftover Shake 'n Bake from home. I was about to take the first bite when I heard a familiar voice from behind me.

"Hey BERKman!"

I turned around and saw the scariest thing I had seen so far.

CHAPTER 11
AN UNEXPECTED FRIEND

"Brett Looger? What are you doing here?"

"What do you think, DORKman? My family moved here over the summer. I ditched yesterday. What the heck is up with this place?"

Brett Looger is the biggest, meanest bully from Deep Valley. You may remember him as the main reason I don't skateboard through puddles to this day.

Brett's eyes darted around the lunch hall like bumblebees. It looked like his mind was on overload, as if there were so many people to beat up, he didn't know where to start.

The good news was that Brett was dressed just like always, with oversized shorts that went down to his ankles, a motocross T-shirt with the sleeves cut off, and a backpack covered in baseball and motorcycle stickers. Brett also had the beginnings of a mustache, but that was because he was turning thirteen soon, having repeated the fourth grade twice.

"Brett, did you do the advance homework they sent you?"

"You think I would do homework before school even started? What do you think I am, a stupid nerd like you, DORKman?"

"Listen, Brett. There's something very wrong with this place." I whispered to him the whole story about the homework coming to life and eating my dog. After I finished, it took a few moments to sink in, but as soon as Brett saw that I was dead serious... he pointed at me and started laughing.

His laughter caught on quick, and in seconds, everyone in the lunch hall was pointing and laughing at me. Then, just as quickly, were back to quietly eating their lunches.

Even Brett was creeped out.

"See what I mean?" he said. "What is up with this place?"

"Just *don't* do the homework," I urged. "And for that matter, don't taste the food either."

Brett turned away with a snort. When he did, I saw a tattoo on the back of his neck that read: *Iron Fist.* Some people called him that because when he hits you, it feels like he's wearing brass knuckles.

*****

I managed to stay quiet and squeak by the rest of day. Sometimes I would look over at Brett and see him doing drawings in his notebook.

That was the one thing the class back at Deep Valley actually liked about Brett. He would draw comic books with skeletons fighting against vampires, werewolves eating ninjas, and other cool stuff like that. He would even make copies for everybody in the class and hand them out Fridays at lunchtime. Eventually, one of them got into the hands of Principal Goodwin. He was disgusted by them and forbid Brett from showing any more of his comics at school.

That was the end of it and Brett looked depressed for a long time. It was no surprise to us when, on the last day of school, Principal Goodwin came out and found his car completely covered in Harley Davidson stickers.

At any rate, I don't think Brett wrote down a single thing Ms. Covenly said all day. He seemed resigned to flunking another grade. Still, it was good to see him drawing again.

At the end of the day, Ms. Covenly told Brett and I to stay behind so she could give us our homework assignments. Brett looked over at me, suspiciously.

The two towers of papers were again stacked neatly on her desk. Ms. Covenly kept an eye on me like a hawk. "All right, Rudy. After your talk with Principal Pooly, I assume you will be doing your homework assignment tonight?"

"Um...no," I said flatly.

Ms. Covenly grimaced at me. Brett seemed shocked, and rather impressed.

"And why not?" she asked angrily.

"If you give me my dog back, I might think about it," I said in complete control.

Brett's eyes widened. He was getting excited at this interchange.

"Well, if that's the case, I suppose the next step will be a conference with your parents. I'm sure they'll be thrilled to hear about your behavior thus far."

At that, she spun me around and stuffed the homework paper in my backpack.

"And Mr. Looger, here is your homework assignment. I look forward to a more productive day from you tomorrow."

"Uh huh," Brett grumbled. Brett and I walked to the pick-up circle. My mom was waiting for me in the SUV.

"Hey, Berkman," said Brett. "How about you come home with me so we can do the homework together? When nothing happens, I want to make sure you're there so I can sock you in the arm. Hah! Just kidding, Berkman." Then he socked me playfully in the arm. It hurt, but I pretended like it didn't.

I ran over and asked Mom if anyone had found Beast. "No. Sorry, Rudy. No one's seen him yet." I wasn't surprised. I told my mom I was going over to Brett's house to do homework. She was so happy that I had made a friend, she quickly agreed.

"Just make sure you're back for dinner by 6:00 p.m.! Love you!" Mom sang, giving me a big embarrassing kiss on the cheek.

Brett snorted as I walked back to him. "Loooove you!" he teased, making a kissy face.

"Where's your parents' car?" I asked.

"No parents. No car," Brett muttered. "I drive myself now."

Brett pointed to a shining blue motocross bike. He tossed me a helmet.

"Let's ride, Berkman."

CHAPTER 12
BRETT'S BIKE

"**W**hoa! When did you get your own bike?" I exclaimed.

"My Grandma got it for me last week," Brett said, proudly. "It was to make me feel better for moving us to this new town."

The bike looked amazing—just like those high-powered dirt bikes that conquer the mountains of dirt and get big air in the X Games. It was a bright deep blue. Brett had already covered it with graphics and stickers. The only strange thing was...

"Why does it have a sidecar?" I asked.

Attached to the side of the bike was a tiny pod, also covered in stickers.

"My Grandma made me get the sidecar so I could drive her around town in it. And if you knew anything about bikes, you'd know they also have sidecar racing called Sidecarcross, which is almost as sick as regular motocross."

"Oh, yeah. I knew that," I said. I knew nothing about bikes.

I strapped on the helmet and hopped in the sidecar. Brett turned on the engine. It made an earsplitting roar as Brett revved the handlebars.

"This is only an 85cc engine!" Brett shouted over the engine's din, so I could barely hear him. "I'm going to save up and upgrade to a 150cc by next summer!"

"Awesome!" I had no idea what he was talking about.

"Hold on!" Brett shouted. In an instant, we were zooming out of the school's parking lot and were flying down the street.

"Whoo-hoo!" I shouted. This was better than any rollercoaster I had been on in my life.

"Do you know who the best athletes in the world are, Berkman?" Brett said to me as he whizzed down the backstreets of Danville.

"Um... basketball players?"

"Nope."

"Soccer players?"

"Nope. Motocross racers. During a race, motocross racers get their heart rate up to around one hundred eighty to one hundred ninety beats per minute and hold it there for about thirty-five minutes. Plus, a racer has to keep complete control of a two-hundred-pound bike, while also maintaining their top speed throughout the race. No other athletes even come close to that level of strength and endurance."

It always amazed me how even someone who flunked two grades like Brett could be so smart about the things they were most passionate about.

"Mark my words, Berkman. In two years time, I'm going to be the junior motocross champion. In three years, I'm turning pro and won't have to do another homework assignment as long as I live. You can even be a member of my team. You know how to replace a chassis?"

"I can really be on your team? I didn't think you even liked me."

"What are talking about? We were always friends, Berkman."

"What about the time you split my skateboard over your knee?"

"Huh? You got mud on my new kicks! What did you expect?"

After a couple miles, Brett pulled the bike to side of the road. To our right was a series of rolling hills, all with brand new houses being built on them. It was a spectacular track housing development, but all of the houses were just wood frames at the moment. There were dozens of tractors, cranes, and bulldozers.

"Why are we stopped?" I asked Brett.

"I feel something moving inside my backpack. See what it is."

Indeed, something looked to be moving inside Brett's backpack. I slowly unzipped it. The sheet of homework shot out with a shriek, then floated down softly into Brett's lap with a small pencil sitting on top of it.

Brett stared at the homework paper. I tried to peer over his shoulder to see what it said. Brett let out a whimper, as if a sudden sickness had swept over him.

"What's wrong?" I asked.

"It's this question," he said. "They want me to write where my mom is."

"That's just like the last question on mine. Only they wanted to know about my grandfather. Just write and see what happens."

At that, Brett turned around and socked me in the arm again.

"Oww! Why'd you do that?"

"I'm not writing that my mom is...is..."

I'd never seen Brett so emotional. Not even when Principal Goodwin took away all his comic books. He wiped his eyes, then turned around in a huff and dropped his face into his hands.

46

"I'm sorry, Rudy. It's just that my mom and dad died in a car crash seven years ago."

Strange. That was the same time my Grandpa Stu went into the mental institution. And the same time Dr. Lyman Yux became mayor of Danville.

"I'm sorry," I said.

"Uh huh. The heck with this. I'm not reading another question."

Brett grabbed the homework in his lap and crumbled it into a ball so fast, I didn't have time to stop him. He tossed the ball of homework as far as he could, then revved the engine on the bike.

"Geez, that's loud!" I yelled.

"That wasn't my bike," said Brett. "I didn't start it yet."

The growling was getting closer and closer. We turned around slowly...

And screamed louder than we ever had before.

 47

CHAPTER 13
A BUMPY RIDE

One of my favorite TV shows has always been "Shark Week" on the Discovery Channel.

There's something about watching a Great White shark, the most ferocious killing machine on Earth, tearing apart its prey between row after row of dental daggers that keeps me hypnotized.

I even made my mom buy me the best shark movie of all time, *Jaws*, on Blu-Ray last summer. I watched it every single day. I was also too afraid to swim in a pool or even take a bath for the whole summer, but it was worth it.

If any career sounded appealing to me at this point in my life, a marine biologist who studied Great White Sharks would be it. Marine biologists, however, always have the protection of a steel shark cage. The moment Brett and I turned around and saw a twenty-foot Great White Shark floating in mid-air, looking back and forth to decide which one of us to eviscerate first, working in my dad's carpet store suddenly seemed like a great career choice to me.

While *my* homework paper had only turned into a vicious mouth, this was obviously an improved version. One designed to eat bigger kids.

Floating in front of us, it looked and moved every bit like a Great White Shark, but was made out of paper, like a horrific work of origami. It was even true to a shark's nature, swimming in circles above us, waiting for the perfect moment to strike.

48

If I learned one thing from Shark Week, it's that there's only one sure way to avoid a shark attack. Get out of the water. Fast.

Brett seemed awestruck by the vision of the giant shark. I whispered sharply: "Get us *out of here.*"

Brett turned to me as if I'd snapped him out of a trance. "You're right. Let's go."

He turned the ignition. Once...twice...it wasn't starting.

The shark lunged toward us.

The third time was the charm. The bike revved. In an instant we were off. The shark missed us by inches, eating a face full of pavement.

That bought us a few seconds as we sped into the distance. The shark gathered itself and came after us even faster.

We were about to enter a neighborhood with heavy traffic and kids on the street. Brett knew we couldn't afford to slow down.

Brett shouted, "Hang on Berkman!" and made a sharp right turn into the housing development lot. We were off road now. Both Brett and the bike were more at home. All around us were countless dirt hills with big houses in the first stages of construction. It must have been the workers' day off, as the grounds seemed deserted.

The shark surged toward us, but Brett stepped on the gas. The back wheels sent mud flying into the shark's face, blinding him momentarily.

We pressed forward, accelerating straight up a dirt hill. We hit the peak and went airborne, soaring thirty feet in the air, then landed safely on the downward slope of the opposite hill. We picked up speed and climbed up the next bigger hill. We soared off its peak, this time forty feet in the air, landing with a thunk on the opposite hill.

"Berkman! Shark report!" Brett ordered.

49

"I turned my head reluctantly, praying I wouldn't be staring into a mouthful of teeth.

The coast looked clear, but then the shark came flying over the hill, thrusting itself in the air like it was leaping through the water for its prey.

"It's right on top of us!" I shouted.

As we came down on top on the last hill, the shark had gained ground and was streaming toward us. I had an idea and shouted to Brett, "Three o'clock!" Brett took my cue and made a sharp right. The shark shot past us again, hurling upward for another near miss.

Brett's sharp turn steered us straight into one the houses under construction. We drove across the wood-planked floor with a clackety-clack sound. Meanwhile, the shark had made a u-turn in mid-air and followed us into the house. The shark burst through the door frame, sending wood shrapnel flying. It was even angrier than before.

With incredible precision and expertise, Brett steered us in and out of empty wood rooms. The clumsy shark had trouble following us and crashed through the planked walls. Onward we sped through the house, like navigating through a giant wooden skeleton where one wrong turn could be our end.

Finally, we burst out the back door. The bike, with me hanging on in the sidecar, skidded across the hilltop, creating a wall of dust behind us. The shark followed moments later, bursting through the back wall of the house in a fury, taking out a support beam with it. The entire wooden structure began collapsing with a thunderous sound. When the beams crashed down, plank after plank of wood began rolling down the hillside.

The shark caught up with us, its fearsome head exploding through the dust cloud behind us. It took a wild snap at me, but I ducked into the pod. Brett reached back and punched it in its nose. Roaring with anger, it zoomed ahead of the bike and swiped the front wheel with its tail. Brett lost control of the bike and it flipped over.

Brett and I were ejected from our seats and went tumbling and

50

somersaulting down the dirt hill. We came to a stop at the foot of the hill. I was bruised, exhausted, and barely conscious. Brett moaned, blood streamed out from cuts on his cheek and shoulder. I felt alert, but was pinned against a pile of wood, unable to move. The ecstatic paper shark swam toward Brett, assured of its victory and imminent meal. The smell of blood no doubt drove it mad with hunger. In desperation, I threw the small pebbles lying around me at the shark, but it was undeterred. It took Brett's feet in its mouth and was starting to ingest him. When suddenly...

A pile of bricks dropped from sky. The bricks landed square on the shark, burying it in a pile ten feet high. In my fuzzy state, I tried to focus my eyes to see where the bricks came from. Above the pile of bricks was a giant steam shovel. There was a man in the steam shovel waving to me. I couldn't tell who it was. He hopped out of the steam shovel and ran over. As he got closer, I immediately recognized the long black hair and thick, curly mustache.

It was Ice Cream Ivan.

He pulled me up from the pile of wood shouting, "Ladies and Gentlemen, let's hear it for Rudy Berkman, who survived a shark attack and a tumble down a hill with barely a bruise or a scratch!"

He then made a noise with his mouth that sounded like a crowd cheering.

I dusted myself off and quickly ran over to Brett. I patted him on the cheek to wake him up. He opened his eyes slowly.

"Berkman? What happened? Am I alive?"

"Yes, we're alive," I said. "This is Ice Cream Ivan. He saved us. The shark is buried under that pile of bricks."

"Boys, that pile of bricks won't hold him for long," warned Ivan. "We'd best make our way out of here. Follow me."

Brett and I followed Ivan over the hills. We seemed to be miles from civilization. Eventually, we came to a cave on the side of a mountain. Brett was pushing his bike over the rocky terrain. We entered the cave. Inside, it looked as if Ice Cream Ivan had set up cozy little home for himself.

"So, you're not just an ice cream man, are you?" I asked Ivan.

"The child prodigy strikes again!" replied Ivan. "Like you said, that would be a very difficult living these days. So instead of one thing, I decided to do, well, everything."

"Everything?" I asked.

"Yes, sir! I'm Danville's Ice Cream Man, its steam shovel operator, its plumber, its hedge trimmer, its morning DJ, its theater critic, and its sole member of the Grand Mustache Society."

"Hold on," said Brett. "Is this your home?"

"Yes, sir. Welcome to Casa de Ivan."

"You live inside a cave? So you're like, a real-life caveman?" laughed Brett.

"Ha! I guess so. Ooga Booga!" Ice Cream Ivan grunted and performed a funny caveman dance.

Brett and I laughed. Minutes ago, I felt like I would never laugh again.

Ivan made a fire. We relaxed and recuperated. Ivan took care of our bruises and scrapes. "I'm glad you found someone you can trust, Rudy. If you two aim to survive here without turning into robots like all the other kids, you're going to have to watch out for each other."

I told Ice Cream Ivan what had happened in school. How my homework had come to life and eaten Beast alive. I pressed Ivan for an explanation of what was going on, but he seemed reluctant to divulge anything.

"Sadly Rudy, I'm not the one to tell you these things, because honestly,

52

I don't know much myself. I wish I could be more help."

Tears welled in my eyes. Why wouldn't he help us? I stammered, "I just... I just want to get Beast back. You have to help me."

Ivan seemed to take pity on me. He stuck his hand through a hole in the cave wall, rustled around, and pulled something out. He stood on a rock and held a flashlight under his face for dramatic effect.

"Rudy, if you truly want your dog back, no matter the cost, there's only one man who can help you rescue him. He is currently imprisoned and must be freed if you are to have the slightest hope. It will be a dangerous and frightful quest, but with your smarts and cunning, there's a slim chance you just might succeed. This is the man you must find and rescue."

Ice Cream Ivan handed me a photograph.

It was a picture of my crazy Grandpa Stu.

CHAPTER 14
THE SLIM-CHANCE RESCUE

"Lucky for you, I know where your Grandpa Stu is!" proclaimed Ivan proudly. "Let the rescue begin."

We piled into Ice Cream Ivan's ice cream truck and hit the road.

I'd never ridden in an ice cream truck before. Brett called shotgun. We loaded his bike in the back of the truck. I (not so reluctantly) sat in back with all the ice cream.

"Go ahead and help yourself to the ice cream!" shouted Ice Cream Ivan from the driver's seat. "Most of it is over five years old anyway."

"Hey, Berkman, toss me an ice cream sandwich," Brett bellowed.

I thought I would be in heaven surrounded by all the ice cream I could ever dream of eating, but I was so cold, the thought of eating frozen food was not very appealing. I wished there were a hot cocoa somewhere.

We exited the border of Danville on a small back road, crossed over the Black Mountains, and in an hour we had reached our destination. It was a big white building with a sign that read: *Gateway Garden Hospital and Mental Health Center*.

Ice Cream Ivan stopped the truck and turned to me with a flourish. "In there, young Rudy Berkman, is where your grandfather is being held captive. Should you enter to retrieve him, it may be the last thing you ever do."

"You're sure he will be able to get Beast back?" I prodded one last time.

"I swear on my mustache." said Ivan, stroking his mustache.

"Then I have to try."

I opened the back doors and jumped out of the truck. I walked slowly toward the two large glass doors at the hospital's entrance. Brett darted in front of me and blocked my way.

"What are you thinking, Berkman? You're just going to walk right in? That'll raise suspicion!"

"I have to at least make sure he's here first. I've never been to visit him. You have a better plan?"

"Uh... not right now... but I'll think of something. I've snuck out of worse places than this."

"You know, you don't have to help me with this Brett. He's my grandpa."

"Look, Berkman. You tried to warn me about the homework. You saved my butt from the shark out there. I would have been eaten alive if it weren't for you. I owe you this."

I nodded at Brett and walked through the glass doors. There was a large reception desk. I had to stand on my tippy-toes to see over it.

"Yes? May I help you?" asked a nurse with a twitching nose and red hair pulled back in a tight bun.

"Hi. Um... is Stuart Berkman here?"

"And who may I ask wants to know?" she replied officiously.

"I'm Rudy Berkman. His grandson."

The nurse's stern manner suddenly became very cheery. "Oh! Rudy Berkman! He talks about you all the time. He'll be so excited you're here. Just a second."

The nurse pressed an intercom button and announced on a p.a. system: "Stuart Berkman, your grandson, Rudy, is here to see you."

Almost immediately, a whole swarm of people came lurching out of doors and peered around from corners and hallways. They were all staring at me.

"What's going on?" I asked nervously.

"Stuart speaks so highly of you, all the patients and staff were beginning to wonder if you actually existed."

Then, from the back of the crowd, I heard a strangely familiar voice.

"Move it! Move it, you! Step aside!"

And then, there he was. Frailer than I remember with a wispy white beard, shaggy white hair, and a face that looked both wise and weathered, like an old farmer who had spent his life in the sun. His eyes blinked hard every time he blinked, like he had to force them down with all his might. The man I hadn't seen since my fourth birthday party, the man who had given me Beast as a birthday present on that fateful day, the man who I told all my friends was dead, was standing in front of me, eyes beaming with love, and I immediately felt an overwhelming guilt for avoiding him all these years.

"Rudy! It's really you! I'm not asleep, am I?"

"No, Grandpa. I'm really here."

"Oh. Well then!" Grandpa sauntered over to me as fast as his old, skinny legs could carry him and gave me a big hug.

"Where's your mom and dad? They didn't tell me you was comin'."

"They're not here."

"Huh? Who'd you come with?"

"Just... um... some friends."

"Friends? Where are they?"

Before I could answer, Brett answered my grandpa's question for him.

Bursting through the glass doors, Brett's bike skidded into the lobby of the hospital, pulling a 180-degree, spinning break.

"Get in the bike! Quick!" yelled Brett.

I pulled my grandpa's hand and jumped into the sidecar.

"Get in with me, Grandpa!" I shouted. "I'll explain later!"

"What the?!" Grandpa was resisting getting into the sidecar.

"Grandpa quick!"

It was too late. Orderlies had run in front of Brett's bike and pulled the keys from the ignition. They pulled Brett off the seat and held him.

The nurse leapt from her station and stormed angrily toward the three of us. "Just what is going on here?"

"Please!" I cried with desperation. "I just need my grandpa for one day. You have to let him go!"

"Rudy, settle down," said Grandpa Stu. "What do you need me for?"

"They took Beast!"

"Who took Beast?"

 57

"I don't know! Ivan said you're the only one who can help me get him back."

"Ivan? You mean, Theater Critic Ivan?"

It was then that Ivan burst through the door with an enormous tray of ice cream strapped around his shoulders.

"Ice Cream! Come get your free Ice Cream!" Ivan proclaimed, throwing ice cream sandwiches, frozen bananas, and creamy popsicles into the air.

Suddenly the lobby was stormed by patients clamoring for the ice cream. The nurse shouted "Great Scott! It's Hedge Trimmer Ivan! The one who escaped ten years ago! Get him!"

The staff was trying to grab Ivan and at the same time restore order with all the hospital patients scrambling for the ice cream. Brett and I looked at one another and saw this was our only chance.

I didn't have time to argue with Grandpa Stu anymore. I shoved him into the sidecar. He fell backwards into it, landing on his bottom. I climbed in with him, Brett snatched the keys from the orderly's hand, leapt on the bike, started the engine, and we took off with a screech.

"Hold on!" screamed Brett.

We flew out the entrance, and as we sped away, the last thing I saw was Ivan being subdued by the hospital staff shouting: "Good luck, Rudy! My show is over! Thank you! Thank you!"

As soon as we were in the clear, Grandpa Stu said to me, "You know, Rudy, I committed myself voluntarily. I could have just signed out and gone with you for the day."

"What?" I shouted in disbelief. "But, Ice Cream Ivan said we had to break you free and rescue you."

"Heh," chuckled Grandpa Stu. "In case you hadn't noticed, that Ivan has a flair for the dramatic."

CHAPTER 15
DON'T OPEN THE FREEZER

As we took the old road through the mountains back into Danville, I told Grandpa Stu everything that had happened. How my first homework assignment had eaten Beast and disappeared. How just hours ago, an even more horrific homework monster had nearly eaten both Brett and me.

Rather than being surprised or not believing me, as I told him the story, Grandpa Stu seemed to grow sadder and sadder.

"I'm sorry, Rudy." Grandpa whispered. "I'm sorry I wasn't there for ya'. You wasn't supposed to be a part of this. We was trying to keep you out. But now it looks like you're in it whether you like it or not."

"In what? You know what's going on in this town?" I was cautiously hopeful that somebody had answers to all the mysteries of this town. Why was everyone always so happy? Why do the kids act like robots? And, of course, why would a homework assignment try to eat me and how could I get my dog back?

"Hey! Where am I taking us?" shouted Brett from the front of the bike.

Grandpa Stu got a good look at Brett for the first time and his jaw dropped.

"Well I'll be. You're Helga Looger's grandson, ain't ya'?"

"Yeah, how did you know?"

 59

"Well, you look just like her is all. Heh! Yeah, me and your Grandma go way back. Just take us to your place. She'll be thrilled to see me. Heh heh!"

"But Grandpa, what about Beast?"

"Just hold your horses. No use rushin' into anything. We'll get your dog back. I'll tell you everything as soon as we're off this road and someplace a little quieter."

We pulled onto Raven Street and parked in front of Brett's house. The cramped quarters of the sidecar were very uncomfortable and my legs had fallen asleep. I had to shake them like crazy before I could stand up.

Brett rang the doorbell and an old woman answered the door. She was plump and weathered with short, poofy gray hair.

She looked straight past Brett and I at the smiling face of Grandpa Stu.

"Hello, Stuart," she grumbled, rolling her eyes.

Grandpa Stu helped himself inside. "Humph," croaked Grandpa Stu, "I would expect a nicer greeting from my own wife."

"Ex-wife. That was a long time ago, Stuart."

"Still feels like yesterday to me. Haven't you missed me, Helga darling?"

"You mean have I missed being run out of town by an angry mob with torches? Have I missed being kicked out of my own order and sleeping in alleyways for years? Have I missed..."

"Okay, Helga, I get the point. You always focus on the negative."

"Wait a minute, wait a minute!" I piped in. "You two were married? Does that mean you're my grandmother? I thought Grandma Martha died before I was born."

"Yeah," Brett injected. "Are you my Grandpa?"

Grandpa Stu and Helga looked over at us and sighed with embarrassment, just now remembering we were there.

"No, Rudy, I'm not your grandmother," said Helga.

"And I ain't your grandfather, Brett."

"I left this sad sack long before he met... Myrtle... Marla...."

"Martha! Her name was Martha!"

"What a catch she was. Not a magical bone in her body."

"Martha did more magic for me than you ever could. Even gave me a son."

"How dare you!" Helga said furiously.

"Bring it," egged on Grandpa Stu. "You don't have the strength you used to. I can take you!"

Brett pulled me aside. "I can't take this anymore. Let's go upstairs. I'll show you my room."

We ran upstairs to a door with a skull-and-crossbones sticker on the front that read: KEEP OUT. Inside the room, posters of motorcycles and baseball players covered the walls.

Brett collapsed on his bed.

"What a day, huh Berkman?"

"Yeah," I said. "Cool posters."

"Thanks," said Brett. "Who's your favorite baseball player?"

"Chet Kingston," I said with no hesitation.

"Really? Well, you'll love this. Check this out."

Brett led me to an umbrella stand next to his closet, but instead of umbrellas, there were at least a dozen baseball bats, both aluminum and wood. He pulled out a wood bat and showed it to me."

"Signed by Chet Kingston. 'To Brett, way to use your head. – Chet.' Pretty cool, huh?"

"How did you get this?

"I was at a game and his bat slipped out of his hands and hit me in the head. I woke up in a hospital bed with this bat sitting next to me. Totally worth it."

"Totally," I said scanning the room awkwardly. "Hey, so... kinda weird that our grandparents used to be married, right?"

"Yeah, does that make us family or something?"

"I don't know. Maybe."

"Cool. I've never had much family except for my grandma. Hey, are you hungry? My grandma makes amazing macaroni."

"Sure!"

We walked back to the bedroom door, but suddenly, Brett's king-size bed tumbled on its side and crashed down right in front of us, blocking our way out the door.

"Oh no," I said. "Oh no."

"What's going on?" said Brett, more scared than I'd ever seen him.

"This is what happened right before my homework ate Beast.

The windows closed shut and locked themselves. We pushed and pushed, but the bed was too heavy to move out of the way.

Then, from behind us, we heard a menacing growl. We turned our heads slowly and saw a dirty sheet of paper slip through the window sill.

It floated in the air, grumbling and growling. A bolt of electricity shot from an outlet. The paper once again transformed into the terrifying paper shark. It looked bruised and haggard, almost falling apart, which somehow made it look even scarier than before.

"It escaped, just like Ivan said it would," I said.

The shark growled furiously as thousands of sharp teeth sprouted in its mouth. Its eyes glowed a fiery red.

"We have no choice but to fight, Berkman. Here." Brett dashed across the room and tossed me a thirty-one inch Easton bat. He held up the signed Chet Kingston.

"Berkman, you get him from the back! I'll take its head!"

I ran to the other side of the room, but the shark stayed focused on Brett. Then, with a sudden thrust of its tail, the shark shot towards Brett with its mouth wide open and teeth ready to chomp.

Brett let out a yell and swung the bat with all his might at the shark's head as if it were a fastball down the plate. KABLAM!

Brett hit it squarely in its lower jaw. The shark jerked back with a shriek of pain. Dozens of its teeth scattered across the floor. The shark backed up towards me in a daze. I jumped into the air, whacking it on its back like it was a floating piñata.

The shark wiggled away from my blows and swam to the corner of the ceiling and wall.

63

"C'mon!" yelled Brett. "Let's finish him!"

We ran beneath the shark and started jumping and swinging our bats, but he shark was too high up for us to land any solid hits.

Suddenly, Brett let out a cry of pain next to me. The dozens of teeth lying on the floor had come to life and were flying into Brett's leg! Blood streamed down his calf.

Brett bravely started to pull the teeth out of his leg and threw them at the shark. That proved an unwise move as the teeth happily planted themselves back in the shark's mouth.

Unfortunately, the thing about sharks is that when they smell blood in the water, that's what sends them into a feeding frenzy. This giant paper shark was no different. Smelling Brett's blood, it darted to the other side of the room with renewed fervor.

With a whip of its tail, it dashed toward us. Brett and I both swung for its head at the same time. This time, however, the shark was prepared, and it opened its mouth as wide as it could and bit down on the bats with such force that they shattered into a thousand tiny pieces as if they were made of glass. With such a bite, our own skulls would have been pulverized.

We were defenseless. We looked around the room, but there was nothing to fend off the shark with. All we had were the measly bat handles. The shark grinned an evil grin and laughed an evil laugh.

Not wasting any time, it lunged toward Brett. At that moment, my Shark Week watching paid off. I knew just what to do. I grabbed the shark by the tip of its nose, where its nerve cluster was located, and squeezed tightly. That put it into a momentary trance, halting the attack.

Both Brett and I used the moment to start screaming for help. "HELP US! HELP!"

We ran to the back of the room and huddled together in preparation for another attack, but just as the shark was coming to, we heard a voice yell, "Clear the doorway!"

All of sudden, a blast of blue energy streamed through the door, straight through Brett's bed. It left a hole just big enough for a kid to crawl through. We looked through the hole and saw Brett's Grandmother Helga standing on the other side with smoke rising from her hands.

"C'mon boys!" she shouted. "I would have been here sooner, but my hearing's not so good."

The shark swam toward us, frantically. Brett took the handle of the bat and threw it in the shark's mouth. The handle got lodged in the shark's throat. It started choking and coughing.

In an act of true unselfishness I will never forget, Brett used the opportunity not to crawl through the hole himself. Instead, he grabbed me by the back of my pants and threw me through the opening, the same way he used to throw me into trashcans.

For the moment, I was safe on the other side of the door. Grandpa Stu was there making sure I was okay. Brett started squeezing himself through next. He was having a tough time, so Helga, Grandpa, and I grabbed his arms and started pulling him out.

Then, Brett screamed a scream I never want to hear again. From inside his room, the shark sank its teeth deep into Brett's legs and was pulling him back inside.

Brett was being pulled backward harder than we could pull him forward.

"Get me out, please!" Brett pleaded.

We pulled and tugged with all our might, but he was slipping away from us. I was having flashbacks of Beast slipping away from me. I was determined not to let it happen again.

"You let go of him, you foul demon!" I heard Brett's grandmother yell with an intensity I'd never heard from an old person. Her hands were beginning to glow blue again.

Then, with a sharp yank, Brett was pulled back into the room.

"Nooo!" we screamed.

Helga pushed me aside and crawled through hole. I tried to crawl in too, but Grandpa Stu held me back. Peering through the hole, I could only see flashes of blue light and hear the sound of energy blasts. Brett was screaming, "Help me Grandma! Help m—" then was silent.

Helga came back through the hole, her forearms riddled with bloody wounds. "Follow me, now!"

We ran down the stairs. "What happened to Brett?" I implored.

"He's gone! We have to save you now."

We were halfway down the stairs when the shark smashed through the bedroom door, sending shards of wood flying. It started chasing us down the stairs.

"It can eat more than one of us?" I huffed.

"It's a shark. It can eat as much as it wants," Helga replied.

Brett's grandmother was clearly not the frail old woman I thought. Grandpa and I could barely keep up with her as we darted through the many rooms and corridors of the house.

The shark was catching up steadily behind us, but was slowed by each sharp turn, crashing into walls, obliterating paintings and cabinets.

Finally, we reached the kitchen. Helga grabbed a big chopping knife and stood in front of me.

I trembled with terror, but fully trusted Brett's grandmother. I heard the air whipping from outside and knew the shark had picked up our scent. It swam slowly through the kitchen door and into the kitchen. I could see its full belly where Brett was now resting.

Helga pulled me over so that we stood in front of the refrigerator/freezer. The shark circled the room, making sure we were cornered.

"Can you blast it?" I whispered.

"No," she whispered back. "Need to recharge. Won't be able to for a while."

The shark faced us head-on, grinning its terrifying grin.

Grandpa Stu pulled a flask out of his pocket and took a quick swig. Suddenly, his arm muscles bulged out like a bodybuilder's. He beat his chest in anger. He ran up to the shark and started punching it with all his might.

It was a tough fight, like two heavyweight boxers going at each other, but the shark knocked Grandpa aside with a whip of its tail and focused on us.

"Get ready," Helga warned.

The shark reared back enjoying the moment, then surged toward us like lightning. I thought this would be the end of me.

But even faster than the shark could move, Brett's grandmother pushed me to the side and opened the freezer door with a flourish.

The shark shrieked as it shot straight into a big bag of ice and turned back into a harmless sheet of paper.

Grandma Helga slammed the freezer door shut and quickly wrote a note that read: "DON'T OPEN THE FREEZER." And stuck it on the door.

"Well," she said, "that was a close one."

I was grateful to be alive, but I couldn't believe she was so upbeat when her grandson had just been eaten alive.

"What about Brett?" I yelled. "He's gone!"

"For now, yes he is," she said. "But now we have the advantage to get him and the rest of the children back."

Grandpa Stu picked himself up and pulled another flask out of his vest pocket, took a sip, and his muscular body went back to normal. I was frozen in shock at everything that had just transpired.

"I suppose," said Grandpa Stu, "it's time we told Rudy the truth, eh, Helga?"

Helga nodded.

And thus would begin the talk that would change my life forever.

CHAPTER 16
THE WAR OF THE ANKARAS

"**W**ell, what do you want to know first?" asked Grandpa Stu.

"First off, why were you in the mental hospital if you aren't really crazy? How did you get buff so quickly? What happened to Brett? How did—

"Okay, Okay..." muttered Grandpa Stu. "It's true that I've been in a crazy house for the last seven years. I agreed to it to make your father happy and keep you safe. Rudy, didn't your father ever tell you about me?

"He said that you're crazy and never to believe a word you say."

Grandpa Stu lowered his head, hurt.

"What about the War of the Ankaras?" Grandpa asked perking up. "Did your dad ever mention that?"

"He told me you were in the military. That's why he had to move so much."

"Well, I guess that's kind of true. But it wasn't the kind of army you know about. It was a magical army! He never said nothin' about it?"

"No. All he ever talks about is carpets."

Grandpa Stu chuckled. "Yes, he was always into them carpets ever since I got him a flying carpet for his fifth birthday."

"Wait," I said. What about Brett? He's—

"He's fine for now," said Grandpa Stu. "Just hear me out a minute."

"But why should I even trust you? You've been in a crazy house for the last seven years."

"Now listen here, boy. I may be lots of things, but crazy I ain't. I'm gonna tell you the truth. Whether you believe it or not is up to you."

Grandpa Stu took a deep breath, stroked his beard, and searched his mind to bring back every detail he could. He looked me in my eyes and put his hand on my shoulder.

"Rudy, there are two kinds of folk in this world: normal, everyday folk and also a few special folk who have what you might call... magical powers."

"Oh! Just like the X-Men. There are humans and mutants."

"Sure. The Hex-Men. So, ya see, us folks with magical powers, we call ourselves Ankaras. Named after the ones who first gave us our powers."

Ankaras? Where had I head that before? That's right! On Sunday when I first met Ice Cream Ivan. He told me everyone in the park was a bad Ankara.

Grandpa continued, "But just like with everyday folk, you got your good Ankaras and you got your bad Ankaras. A long time ago, it used to be that all Ankaras were good. We lived by a very strict code. In fact, before someone became an Ankara, you had to take an oath to follow three rules: Number One: You must keep your powers secret from everyday folk. Number Two: You must never use your powers to hurt or kill any kind of folk, magical or not. And Number Three: You cannot make someone an Ankara who is not part of an Ankara family or if they don't want to be one."

"Make someone an Ankara? What do you mean?" I asked.

"The truth is, Rudy, just about everybody has some special ability or magical power locked away deep inside them. Take me. After I was told the Magic Words, suddenly all the plants and rocks sounded like they was singin' to me. They was tellin' me the deepest secrets of their beings. With practice I was able to mix all those things into magical potions!"

"Like the potion of strength you just drank?" I asked.

"That's right, Rudy. But like I said, everyone has their own special power. To bring it out, you have to be told the Magic Words. When the first Ankaras were given the Magic Words, they realized that the way folks are; well, they reckoned they'd be using their powers to do more bad than good. So they kept the Magic Words a secret, and only made the most honorable, most good folks into Ankaras. And once all the good folks were chosen, they had to keep the magical powers within their families."

"But how could they be sure?" I asked. "Wouldn't kids just turn all their friends into Ankaras?"

"Good question, Rudy. They made sure that wouldn't be happening because only two Ankaras at any one time know the Magic Words. They're called the Guardians – the leaders of all Ankaras. A Guardian whispers the Magic Words into a new Ankara's ear when they're sleeping. That way they don't remember 'em."

"So who are they? Who are the Guardians alive today?"

"Oh come on, Rudy. I think you already know the answer to that question."

He was right. I guess I just didn't want it to be true. "Dr. Lyman Yux."

"That's right, Rudy. Can you guess the second?"

"Hmm. Principal Pooly?"

"Pooly? Ha! No, Rudy. It's me. Dr. Lyman Yux and me."

71

"And a fine decision that was," muttered Helga, sarcastically. "Look what's happened while your grandfather's been running things. Nearly all the good Ankaras have vanished or been killed and the bad Ankaras have taken over the city."

"You hush up, Helga. If it wasn't for me there'd be none of us left at all. That's for sure!"

"Tell me what happened," I prodded, separating them once again.

"Well, I'd say about twenty years ago, all us Ankaras were living in peace right here in Shallow Creek. Then, one day, Dr. Lyman Yux gets it in his head that us Ankaras shouldn't be content just livin' together in peace and enjoyin' our powers for ourselves. He thought we should be usin' our powers for no good. To rule over the everyday folk."

I gasped. Things were starting to become clear.

"You can imagine what happened next. About half the Ankaras agreed with Dr. Yux and went over to his side. Even changed their names to end in 'LY', signifying their allegiance to Lyman Yux."

Ms. Covenly... Principal Pooly... the Waverlys. It checked out.

"The other half sided with me. We wanted to stick to the code. We thought it was wrong to use our magic to get power over others. That began the War of the Ankaras. The war went on more than ten years. The bad Ankaras wanted to get rid of all us good ones so we wouldn't stop them from taking over the world."

"And they won?"

"Yes, Rudy. Real life isn't like the movies or your fantasy books. The evil they were willing to do was no match for us Ankaras with a conscience. Very few survived. The bad Ankaras declared victory seven years ago and changed the name of the town from Shallow Creek to Danville. A deliberate choice if you ask me, seeing as if you rearrange the letters in Danville, it spells Evil Land."

"But what can we do if the war is already over?" I asked.

"The war is not completely over, Rudy. They failed in one mission."

"What mission?"

"To kill you."

I felt the back of my throat go dry. "To kill me? Why would they want to kill me? I don't have any powers."

"That's right, Rudy. But you have one great advantage. Your father did not become an Ankara. I pleaded with him time and again, but he wanted to live a normal life, be a carpet salesman, and raise a family. That was his choice. I kept to my oath. But because he never got his powers, all of his powers will go to you, including the ones you already have hidden inside you. Rudy, you will be one of the most powerful Ankaras alive. In fact, there will be only one Ankara equal to you in power."

"Let me guess. Dr. Lyman Yux."

"Right you are. Rudy, you have been our only hope for a long time. When I was around, I protected you as long as I could. Everyone thought I was crazy. Nobody except your father trusted me around you. So, to make everyone happy, I let myself be committed to the crazy house on the condition that your family change its name and move far, far away. It also kept you safe cause I couldn't be tellin' you the Magic Words while I was locked up. Without powers, they didn't consider you a threat."

"I didn't know we changed our name."

"It's true. Years before you was born, everyone in the family changed their name from Billings to Berkman."

"But if it's so dangerous, why would my dad move us back here?"

"Honestly, I don't know. That's something I'm hoping to find out myself. As soon as I got word that you were moving to Danville, I wrote to

Helga that things were about to get bad again. She's been watching over you this whole time."

"The mailbox!" I exclaimed. "You're the one who broke our mailbox before we moved in so I wouldn't get the homework assignment."

"That's right," said Helga. "Unfortunately I couldn't keep watch on you all the time as Brett is quite a handful himself."

That reminded me. "What are we going to do about Brett? And what has been going on with all the kids in this town? Why do they act like robots?"

Grandpa Stu and Helga let out a deep breath. Helga muttered, "Honestly, we don't know what kind of spell the children are under or why. But we're going to find out and try to put a stop to all this. Now that we have this evil homework under our control, we can use it to find the evil Ankaras' lair and get Brett and your dog back."

My eyes started to well up, thinking of the terrible things the evil Ankaras might be doing to Beast. Grandpa came over and hugged me.

"Grandpa Stu, why haven't the evil Ankaras just killed me if I'm the only one who can defeat them?"

"I don't know that either, Rudy. Maybe that cursed homework was a lazy first attempt. Or, seein' as you have so much potential, maybe they want to make you one of them."

I walked toward the window in shock at these revelations. The sun was setting on the horizon. Here I was, finally getting to be chance to live out my dream of being a superhero, just like in the comic books I love. Only this was nothing like the comic books where the good guys always win. Just my luck, the good guys had already been defeated by the bad guys. I was the last, desperate hope for defeating an entire city of supervillains. Oh, and I didn't even have my powers yet.

Something tells me Superman never had it this rough.

"You want to know a secret?" Grandpa whispered. "I told the Magic Words to that dog before I gave it to you on your fourth birthday. I made it so his powers will come out when you're in danger. That pooch will be doin' anything to protect you."

"Will I ever see Beast again?" I asked, my voice shaking.

"Don't worry. We'll get him back. And Helga darling, where were you while my grandson's dog was being eaten alive?"

"Probably cooking dinner for Brett. Boys have to eat, you know."

Suddenly, there was a loud bang from inside the freezer. The freezer door whipped open right into Helga's face, knocking her out cold.

CHAPTER 17
WHAT'S IN THE BOX

"Get down, Rudy!" Grandpa Stu yelled.

I ducked into a small cupboard underneath the grimy kitchen sink. I opened the door a crack and peeked through, expecting to see the horrific shark ready to devour us.

To my surprise, the homework paper had not reformed into the shark. It had become a paper airplane zipping around the room like a fly, bashing into windows, trying desperately to find a way out.

Grandpa Stu found a small cardboard box and was jumping around the kitchen trying to catch it. "Get out from there, Rudy. I have an idea."

"What's it doing?" I asked while crawling out.

"It's being summoned back to its master. This is our chance to finally get some answers."

The paper plane zipped by my head. With an instinctive swipe of my hand, I swatted it to the ground. Grandpa Stu dove onto the floor, covering the plane with the small box.

The plane pounded against the walls of the box trying to escape, but Grandpa sat on top of it, not letting it break free.

"Rudy, we're going to have to let the paper plane go. Then, we follow it."

"But the one that ate my dog flew away so fast, there's no way we could keep up."

"Fast? Feh! Rudy, you gotta start thinking like an Ankara."

At that, Grandpa Stu pulled out a flask from his right pocket.

"Rudy, I ain't gonna tell you what this does, 'cause you'll just get too scared to drink it. What we're gonna do is open the kitchen door, then both take a sip. You'll figure for yourself what to do from there."

As I walked over to open the kitchen door, it suddenly dawned on me how incredibly weird my life had become. There I was, following the orders of my old, withered Grandpa, who had spent the last seven years in an insane asylum and was presently wrestling with a cardboard box. An old lady was lying unconscious on the floor from a vicious refrigerator injury. I was about to drink a mysterious potion in the hopes that it would help get back my dog and my only friend in town, both of whom were eaten alive by unrelenting, monstrous sheets of mutant homework. Not to mention the fact that I was apparently the centerpiece in a decades-old supernatural war that was about to re-erupt.

Three days ago, my biggest problem was being fifty cents short for the new issue of X-Men.

After opening the door, I slowly walked back to Grandpa Stu. He held out a silver flask in his right hand that was marked only with an X.

Grandpa's voice trembled from the vibrations of the box he was smothering. "J-J-Just take a s-s-s-sip. That's all a y-y-y-young m-man n-n-needs."

I reached out and took the flask, somehow knowing that once I took a sip, there would be no turning back.

CHAPTER 18
FOLLOW THAT GLIDER

Besides *Jaws*, another one of my favorite movies is *Honey, I Shrunk the Kids*. Like *Jaws*, it came out before I was born. My Aunt Jenny streamed it with us on my eighth birthday. It was about a family of kids who get shrunk to the size of insects by their crazy inventor dad and have to survive a jungle of horrors in their own backyard just to make it back home.

After seeing the movie, I realized I had never thought that there could be entire worlds and epic battles going on right in the grass of my own backyard. I found a magnifying glass and eagerly started searching between every blade for bugs, worms, or neighborhood kids who may have shrunk.

The best thing I ever saw was an actual butterfly emerging from its cocoon on the thorny stem of Mom's rose bush. At the time, I wished I could shrink down like the kids in the movie and ride on a butterfly's back. But, like I said before, these things aren't supposed to actually happen.

I didn't so much feel myself shrinking as much as the world around me seemed to get bigger and bigger. My clothes became looser and looser until they draped on top of me and I realized I was half the size of the tag on my collar!

"What's happening to me?!" I buzzed in a panic. Wait. I buzzed?

I looked at my legs. I had six of them. They were skinny and black with long, sticky hairs. I turned my head all the way around. Wings on my back! Could it be?

I was a fly!

My wings turned on like a chainsaw and I shot into the air! I darted around the kitchen like a... well, like a fly! While I was figuring out how to work my wings, beneath me, I saw Grandpa Stu take a big chug from the flask. In a flash, he became a big old nasty horsefly!

As soon as Grandpa Stu's weight was lifted from the box, the paper airplane blasted out of it.

Grandpa the horsefly flew over to me like a puttering old car. I still recognized his general facial features in the face of the fly. I could only wonder how I must look.

"Follow that glider, Rudy! It's flying out the door!" Grandpa the horsefly buzzed at me.

"Okay, Grandpa." Amazingly, I could also speak, but in a high-pitched whir that sounded like a dentist's drill.

With a zip and a whip, I dashed toward the glider. It had just found the open door and shot through Helga's backyard.

With Grandpa by my side, we followed the glider flying so quick the human eye probably couldn't see us. I felt like I had the heightened reflexes and senses of Spider-Man. We whizzed through the neighbors' yards at breakneck speed – zipping between tree branches, whooshing through chimney smoke, skipping across swimming pools, bolting through barbecues, and sweeping through swing sets!

Then, the glider made a sharp left turn onto the neighborhood streets, flying right at car level. Was it trying to get us squashed?

The glider weaved between oncoming traffic in an effort to shake us. Getting around the compact cars wasn't too difficult, but when a massive semi came plowing my way, I came just centimeters from becoming bug juice on its windshield!

The glider made a sharp right turn at the end of Newton Street and headed toward the forest.

Bellway Forest is a dark, foreboding entanglement of old oak trees with sharp, draping branches and piercing leaves. It was the kind of place where nightmares come from.

I was flying through the thickness of razor-like branches in almost total darkness.

My heightened sense of smell and the sensitivity of the tiny hairs on my body gave me a clearer picture of my surroundings than sight ever could, especially at our screaming velocity.

In front of us, the soaring glider was an amazement in itself. Any glider I ever threw would inevitably do an immediate nosedive onto the ground or fly the opposite direction I threw it and get stuck in a tree, but this glider was constantly changing shapes – spreading completely flat, rolling into a cigar, and squeezing into a ball to break through weak twigs.

Finally, there was a clearing ahead of us. Like racecars down the final straightaway, we sped down the path toward a light source.

We escaped the forest and arrived at our destination.

Danville Reformatory.

"This is my school!" I shouted, as Grandpa the Horsefly puttered along behind me.

"Well, swat me down! This used to be the home base of the evil Ankaras during the War."

Now in a more open space, we distanced ourselves from the glider, but kept a close eye, or hundreds of eyes as they were, focused on the paper plane as it made its way toward the school playground.

Here, the glider finally slowed down. It started flying in leisurely circles above the merry-go-round that was surrounded by a sandpit.

Grandpa and I perched ourselves on a smooth metal bar atop the slide, absorbing all we could in the dim light.

Abruptly, there was a great gust of wind. We clung with all our stickiness to the slick surface. The wind began swirling until a small tornado formed above the merry-go-round. All the sand in the sandpit lifted high into the air.

Glowing numbers were revealed underneath the sand. They circled the merry-go-round like numbers on the face of clock, only these went from one to sixteen. Then, the merry-go-round began spinning all by itself, three times around to the left, twice to the right, and once again to the left.

It was clear what the merry-go-round actually was. Just like on my locker, this merry-go-round was actually a combination lock.

Grandpa whispered, "Rudy, whatever happens, just follow my lead."

There was a loud clanking of metal, gears turning, chains grinding. The merry-go-round rose upward. Red light streamed out from underneath it.

Then, the glider shot out from the swirl of the tornado and darted underneath the merry-go-round.

"Now, Rudy!"

The merry-go-round was lowering back down and the tornado was spitting out all the sand it was holding. Blinded by the sandstorm, I followed the sound of Grandpa's buzz in front of me as we flew into the mysterious red light.

The merry-go-round sealed shut ominously above us.

CHAPTER 19
FLY TRAP

I still was not used to the fractured imagery of my fly eyes. I saw a kaleidoscope of orange and red light. The bustle of movement in the room made it hard to get a firm sense of what was going on around me.

I smelled burning candles. The smoke made it difficult and unpleasant to breathe. I also sensed at least thirty different bodies in the room, each with its own unique, pungent breath. They all looked to be wearing black cloaks. Excited chatter echoed all around.

Grandpa and I planted ourselves in a dark corner on the wall. Fortunately, we had not been noticed, yet.

Suddenly, all the lights cut out except for a single blue beam in the middle of the room. The beam highlighted a large gridiron cage. Inside the cage, the glider was cruising in slow circles.

Then, the chanting began. First as a low hum, then rising to a high note that could have broken glass. Then, just as quickly, dropping down to a guttural grunt.

As this frightening dirge continued, the glider in the cage began changing shape back into the twenty-foot Great White Shark. Strangely, I felt no fear. I was entranced by the chanting and actually felt rather at ease. In fact, I had the urge to fly into the cage with the shark. It suddenly looked very friendly to me.

I turned on my wings and dislodged my sticky feet from the wall.

"Rudy! Get back here!" huffed Grandpa the horsefly. "Those are *evil* Ankaras down there!"

But it was too late. I was buzzing my way toward the shark cage. If it wasn't for the loud bark that rang through the room, I might have become shark food.

I knew that deep, beagle bark anywhere. I didn't even have to see him. Beast was somewhere nearby.

I took a big sniff to see if I could locate him. I picked up the faint smell of his fur and dog breath, but it didn't seem to be coming from this room.

Beast's bark broke the rhythm of the chanting and the cloaked figures around the shark cage pouted in frustration.

"I thought we were going to put a muzzle on that mutt!" exclaimed a familiar voice.

Another familiar voice piped in, "Hach! What do we do this pointless chant for? Can't we just get on with this? I have a whole cauldron full of mush that's losing its potency for lunch tomorrow."

Lunch tomorrow? Of course, that was the horrid lunch lady, Mrs. Krimbly! The other voice was Principal Pooly!

An outburst of bickering broke out amongst the group. The clamor was quickly hushed by a thunderous pounding from the front of the room.

There, a figure in a sparkling silver cloak rapped his long scepter on the ground.

"Silence!" the figure commanded.

A red crystal atop the scepter emitted a fiery glow. Even with my fly eyes I recognized the face—the piercing eyes, the long white hair, the scary eyebrows...

It was Dr. Lyman Yux.

Red light slithered out of his scepter like a snake. The light weaved its way around the circle of evil Ankaras.

A tall, handsome Ankara cried out, "No! Please don't!"

But it was too late. The red light slunk between every Ankara's lips, and out popped their mouths! Dozens of mouths darted in the air, looking like my grandma's dentures, snapping away and laughing with glee at their newfound freedom.

"If you can't control your mouths," spoke Dr. Yux with his commanding voice, "I will control them for you."

Grandpa quit calling my name and flew in front of me.

"What are you thinking, boy? If just one of them caught a quick gander of you, they'd fry you in mid-air!" He flew into me repeatedly trying to knock me back to the safety of the dark wall.

At that moment, I was more afraid of getting chomped by the disgusting mouths. I returned to the top corner of the stone ceiling with Grandpa.

I must admit it was quite funny seeing all those nasty Ankaras moaning like confused sea lions. Some of them were jumping up trying to grab their teeth back, but their teeth would just bite their fingers, cackle, and fly away.

Despite the amusement in front of him, Dr. Yux kept a stern expression on his face. Eventually, he waved his scepter. The teeth flew back into the Ankaras' mouths and the red light vanished back into Dr. Yux's scepter.

"Hey, these aren't my teeth!" bellowed Mrs. Krimbly.

"That's because they're my teeth!" exclaimed the tall, handsome

84

Ankara. "I want my teeth back! Not these rotten fangs."

Dr. Yux flashed a smile, speaking with delight: "We'll see how many women will kiss you now, Marcus."

The throng burst into laughter at the handsome Ankara, who I suppose was named Marcus. He hung his head shamefully and pursed his lips, which made the other Ankaras laugh all the harder.

Mrs. Krimbly smiled brightly, showing off her new perfect teeth to Mr. Krimbly standing next to her. "Well, Foggy, what do you think?"

Mr. Krimbly, a surprisingly nice looking man, reached out and felt his wife's new teeth. "Verrry nice," he said. Judging by his foggy white eyes and cane, it seemed Mr. Krimbly was blind as a bat.

"Enough of this," spoke Dr. Yux. "It is getting late. Let us skip ahead to the binding."

Applause broke out amongst the Ankaras. "All hail Dr. Lyman Yux!" "Your wisdom is unparalleled, Dr. Yux!"

The Ankaras' focus again turned to the shark swimming circles in the cage. Dr. Yux stepped forward and extended his scepter with its glowing crystal between the bars of the cage. The shark became entranced by the crystal and swam towards it while Dr. Yux intoned these words:

"Kellem Kolara, Kellem Collaws,

Release these boys from your mighty jaws."

At that, the shark broke into a fit of heaving and hacking that sounded like my neighbor's cat coughing up a fur ball. It bucked back and forth like an accordion and soon the head of Brett began to emerge.

As if being reborn, Brett slid out of the shark's mouth covered in slimy goo, landing with a plop on the floor of the cage. He was dazed but managed to stand up. He was wearing gray shorts and a white collared

85

shirt. The unofficial school uniform minus the red tie.

"Where am I? What's going on?" Brett asked fearfully.

"Do not be afraid child," cooed Dr. Yux. "You are in a safe place. We will bring you back home shortly. All you have to do is put on this red tie and be on your way."

"Hey. I know you. You're that freaky mayor of this town. Well let me tell you, Brett Looger doesn't wear a tie for you or *anybody*."

Dr. Yux smiled warmly. "Very well then. You shall sleep here for the night. But I'm afraid your roommate isn't a very pleasant fellow."

Brett followed Dr. Yux's eyes and turned his head. He was face to face with the hungry shark again. All the memories flooded back in his mind and Brett screamed in terror. "Let me out of here! Please!"

"You're welcome to come right out and go straight home... as soon as you put on this tie."

Brett didn't even want to turn around again to evaluate his options. He reluctantly reached through the cage and took the pre-tied tie from Dr. Yux's hand. He dropped the tie down his neck, pushed it under his collar, and cinched the knot upwards.

At that moment, Brett's eyes glazed over. His body lost its looseness and attitude. He seemed to turn into a robot before my eyes.

Dr. Yux spoke, "As you have willingly bound yourself with this tie, so are you now bound to me in servitude. From this day forward, you will obey all orders from Dr. Lyman Yux and do exactly as you are told. Is this understood?"

"Yes, Dr. Yux."

"Whom do you serve?"

"Dr. Lyman Yux."

"Very good. You shall return home now and never tell anyone what has happened tonight."

"Yes, Dr. Yux."

Dr. Yux opened the cage. As Brett stepped out, the Ankaras cheered and whistled their approval. Then, my neighbors, Alan and Barbara Waverly, took Brett by the hand and said, "C'mon, Brett. We'll take you home." And the three left together.

So this is how it all happened.

"Now, release the other boy," Dr. Yux commanded to the shark.

The shark shook its head.

"You have no other boy within you?"

The shark shook its head again.

"Athena!" yelled Dr. Yux.

Ms. Covenly stepped forward, trembling in fear.

"Athena, you said that Brett and Rudy would be together after school."

"But they were together!" Ms. Covenly asserted. "I even saw Rudy get into Brett's sidecar."

She was spying on me! At least Ms. Covenly was getting into trouble, having a taste of her own medicine.

"These homework assignments are not easy to enchant, Athena. You have wasted a great deal of my time."

"I said from the beginning we shouldn't enslave him. He's the grandson of Stuart Billings. He should be killed like the rest of them."

"No more of this. Only if we can get to him before his grandfather does will we finally have the power to put the Great Plan into effect."

I whispered to Grandpa, "The Great Plan? What is he talking about?"

Grandpa shrugged his fly shoulders.

Suddenly, the shark began thrashing about the cage.

"What is it?" asked Dr. Yux of the shark.

In a manic effort, the shark began forcing itself to change shape.

"I have a bad feeling about this, Rudy," whispered Grandpa. "Let's find a way out of here."

Below us, the shark had changed itself into a large paper fly. It buzzed its wings and thrust back and forth against the top of the cage.

"I see," said Dr. Yux.

With a grand spreading of his arms, Dr. Yux flooded the room with light. Grandpa and I were buzzing directly above the cage, trying to find a small crack in the ceiling.

"There they are!" shouted a short Ankara with huge, bulging eyes.

We were seen.

"Fly for it, Rudy!" Grandpa shouted.

I zipped away in a mad rush, but was caught in a beam of light. I couldn't move, as if I were in the grasp of a tractor beam. Beside me, I saw that Grandpa was caught in a separate beam of light, both stemming from

Dr. Yux's scepter.

Dr. Yux lowered us into the shark cage while chanting these words:

"Kellem Corso, Kellem Olar

Become the people that you are."

In a painfully speedy transformation, Grandpa and I both changed back to our human selves. We landed hard on the iron floor of the cage, completely naked.

The Ankaras turned their heads away in disgust, I guess from seeing Grandpa Stu.

A beam of light shot from Yux's scepter, and we were instantly clothed in his trademark gray suit and white shirt, minus the tie.

We were hopelessly trapped. The paper fly buzzed about, laughing in our faces. Dr. Yux glared with devilish eyes, red mist seeping from his scepter like steam from a boiling pot.

All around us, the order of Ankaras wore grins of evil anticipation.

CHAPTER 20
BLUFFERS

"**W**ell, well, well. My old friend, Stuart Billings."

"It's Berkman now, you limey buffoon."

"Yes, of course. *And* your grandson, Rudy. Who knew we had such distinguished guests with us?"

Dr. Yux could barely contain his excitement. The Ankaras cackled with eagerness to see what Dr. Yux was going to do.

"Let us go, Lyman, or you'll be sorry," warned Grandpa.

Dr. Yux finally let out the enormous laugh he had been holding in.

"Ha! Ha! Ha! Really, Stuart. You were no match for me during the War, and you're certainly no match for me now against my entire order."

"Maybe not, Lymey." Dr. Yux grimaced hearing Grandpa's nickname for him. "But Rudy here is more powerful than you could ever dream of being. With one word he could wipe you all out if I tell him to."

I turned my head and looked at Grandpa Stu in confusion. "Go with me, Rudy," he whispered under his breath.

I turned back to Dr. Yux and gave him a smirk that said: That's right. I could wipe you out.

Dr. Yux glared at me with his piercing eyes, dissecting me, but I didn't lose my confidence. The Ankara's sickening smiles were replaced with worried expressions.

"I don't see the Mark of the Magic Words on him, Stuart."

"Of course not," cackled Grandpa, "I had him drink a potion that hides it."

Dr. Yux chuckled, "I simply don't believe you, Stuart. If he could wipe us out, he would have done it already."

"Not a chance, Lymey. I don't want my Rudy to be a murderer like you, unless he has no other choice to defend himself."

Dr. Yux lowered his head and rubbed his temples. He mumbled to himself incoherently as the hairs of his scary eyebrows began dancing and squiggling on their own, like snakes on the head of Medusa.

I turned around and whispered in Grandpa Stu's ear, "What's the plan?"

Grandpa whispered back, "You have to get them to bring Beast in here."

I started to sweat as I noticed the homework still flying around the cage in its giant fly shape.

Then I heard it. *Woof! Woof!* It was Beast. He must have picked up my scent.

"Beast!" I cried. "You have my dog!" I growled at Dr. Yux.

"That's right. It is your fleabag, isn't it? Perhaps we should prepare a doggy stew for tonight?"

Yux and the rest of the Ankaras laughed.

I shut them up, shouting, "You better give me back my dog right now, or I will wipe you all out."

It was a daring bluff on my part, but right now all the Ankaras knew was that Grandpa had gotten to me first. For all they knew, he could have told me the Magic Words. If so, I would be as powerful, if not more so, than Dr. Yux.

Dr. Yux flashed a sick, phony smile. "Very well, Rudy. Grubly, bring in Rudy's mutt."

A short, fat man, barely taller than me, with a flat skull and black robes, wheeled in a small iron cage. Inside was Beast, his paws chained to the bars. Grubly quickly wrapped a muzzle on his snout to stop his barking.

Our eyes met and he let out a series of yelps that burst through his clenched, muzzled teeth.

"What did you do to him? Untie him *right now*," I demanded.

"Come now, Rudy. If you're so powerful, I'm sure you can free him yourself with a snap of your fingers. Go right ahead. I won't stop you."

He was on to me. I was frozen.

"Ha! Rudy doesn't need to show off for you, Lymey. He's too good a kid."

"Maybe. Or maybe Rudy doesn't have any powers. Maybe you haven't even told him the Magic Words, Stuart."

"Don't be ridiculous. Of course I told him."

"Or maybe after years of living in dumpsters, you forgot the Magic Words, Stuart. Maybe that's why you never told them to your son."

"Horse pucky! Don't you listen to his lies, Rudy. You go ahead and use

92

your powers if you want to."

I shot a look at Grandpa. He just winked back at me.

"*Enough!*" Dr. Yux's voice shook the walls and rattled the cage. "You cannot scare me anymore, Stuart. Before I kill you, you are going to watch Rudy bind himself in servitude to me. I will raise him as my own grandson. With you gone, there will be no more interferences with the Great Plan."

The Ankaras burst into applause and cheering.

"You raise your scepter, it will be the last thing you ever do," Grandpa snarled, baring his teeth. But we were out of bluffs. They weren't buying it.

Dr. Yux raised his scepter in the air, pausing for a quick moment.

When we did nothing to stop him, a red beam of light shot out of Yux's scepter right at Grandpa Stu.

CHAPTER 21
TRANSFORMATION

The red beam of light whizzed past Grandpa's head and hit the enormous paper fly.

The fly began glowing red as Dr. Yux chanted frightening sounds in unison with the other Ankaras.

Beast barked furiously, trying to distract the Ankaras, but they were too loud and too focused.

The paper fly began changing its shape. It became larger and larger and LARGER. A mouth full of sharp jaws formed. Two horrible fangs, at least a foot long, sprouted from its terrible gums. Finally, a ten-foot body took shape with a cat-like tail and paws with three-inch claws.

I'd seen enough pictures in pre-historic animal books to know what I was looking at.

It was a Saber-Tooth Tiger.

The tiger growled ferociously as the Ankaras cheered the magic of Dr. Yux. Grandpa and I huddled in the corner of the cage.

"Devour them!" urged Dr. Yux.

The tiger's bubbling drool puddled on the floor of the cage. It smelled our fear and reared back to pounce.

"Grandpa, do something," I pleaded.

"Listen, Rudy. When that tiger pounces, you just scream for your life."

That wasn't the response I was hoping for, but there wasn't time to come up with anything better. The tiger leaned on its hind legs then leapt towards me, its jaws gaping wide enough to swallow me whole.

I closed my eyes and screamed for my life.

CHAPTER 22
TRANSFORMATION: PART II

Everything was silent.

"This is it. I'm dead," I thought.

I was too scared to open my eyes. Who knew where I would be. Especially considering that almost every night I scraped the vegetables off my plate onto the floor for Beast to eat up.

Then, I heard Grandpa Stu whisper, "Rudy, open your eyes."

I was still too scared. I didn't want to see half my body missing.

"Rudy, look!"

I opened my eyes and looked straight ahead.

In front of my face was a gigantic, furry arm.

At the end of the gigantic, furry arm was a gigantic, furry hand. And in the gigantic, furry hand was the neck of the gigantic, Saber-Tooth Tiger. It was wriggling helplessly in the hand's powerful grip.

"Ha, Ha! You made it happen, Rudy!" squealed Grandpa.

Made what happen? I turned around and was greeted with a face-full of fur. But not just any fur. I'd know that fur anywhere. It was Beast. I crawled backward and couldn't believe what I was seeing.

Beast really was a *Beast*. Standing at least nine feet tall, powerfully built, and sporting fearsome teeth, Beast looked like a towering, furry Sasquatch. In fact, he wasn't that far off from Beast of the X-Men, except instead of being all blue, he still had his S'mores-colored fur and floppy ears.

Behind Beast, the iron cage that held him as a dog was broken apart in pieces.

Snarling with rage, Beast smashed the Saber-Tooth Tiger against the bars of the cage over and over again. It made the entire room shake. Soon the fearsome tiger was nothing but a pile of shredded paper on the floor.

Beast let out a triumphant sound that was something between a roar and his deep beagle howl. I'm sure the noise was meant to be terrifying, but it turned out just sounding kind of funny. Nonetheless, his point was made.

Dr. Yux backed up against the wall. The Ankaras gathered around him, begging him to protect them from Beast.

"What is this, Stuart!?" exclaimed Dr. Yux.

"Just a little exhibition of what a good potion and the Magic Words will do for a young pup."

Beast bent apart the bars of the cage and Grandpa and I crawled out and stood behind him.

Dr. Yux tried to catch us off guard. He shot a red beam at Beast from his scepter. The beam bounced off of Beast's chest and ricocheted onto Marcus, the handsome Ankara. Marcus' body started twitching and vibrating. Then, he transformed into a billy goat.

Marcus "baaa-ed" in disgust.

All at once the other Ankaras unleashed a barrage of attacks on Beast, but he was invincible. Lightning bolts, laser beams, darts, arrows, and acidic spit were all deflected back at the Ankaras as if they were fighting against a mirror.

While the Ankaras were busy dodging their own projectiles, Beast lunged toward Dr. Yux in a furious attack. Dr. Yux waved his scepter in a grand motion, forming a glowing red energy shield around him and the rest of the Ankaras. Beast pounded on the shield with all his might, making the Ankaras scream with fright, but the shield held up.

"Rudy," whispered Grandpa, "we gotta get out of here before Beast's transformation wears off."

Wears off? Darn. For a second I thought I was going to have the coolest pet in the world. Well, I guess I still will.

"Beast!" I commanded, "take us home."

Beast looked at me with the same acknowledgement as if I had told him to fetch his ball.

He scampered over with a grin on his face and his tongue hanging out. He pulled Grandpa and I against his body with his right arm.

"Up!" I yelled, pointing upward.

Beast squatted down and then sprang upward with momentous force, his left fist aiming skyward. We burst out of the lair through the merry-go-round, which must have shot upward a hundred feet in the air!

We landed in the playground with a thunk. Beast began running back home, still holding us tight against his furry body.

We reached Bellway Forest and plowed through the dense foliage. Beast must have been annoyed by all the sharp sticks and piercing leaves, so he leapt to the top branches of the canopy. Gripping Grandpa and myself in one arm, Beast swung from branch to branch with his free arm, flying as fluidly and gracefully as a spider-monkey. It was so much fun, for a moment I forgot we were running away and almost asked Grandpa if we could go back and do it again.

As we neared the end of Bellway Forest, Beast started shrinking fast. He jumped back to the forest floor. After setting us down, he hunched over and began running alongside us on all fours until he was the same old Beast the beagle again.

Grandpa and I were running barefoot (having thrown our shoes at the tiger). The sharp, fallen leaves stung and sliced our feet, but our adrenaline carried us onward.

"We can't go back to your house, Rudy. They'll come looking for us there."

"Then where do we go?" I asked.

"There's one safe place. I'm just hopin' it's still there."

We burst out of Bellway Forest and breathed a sigh of relief, but there was still no time to rest. Instead of making a right turn into the suburbs, we made a left and sprinted toward town.

Beast was having trouble keeping up with his short legs, so I carried him against my body just like he had done with me only minutes ago.

"Here it is, Rudy."

We stopped at a storefront in the middle of town. It was Carpet Diem. My dad's store.

"This is where Dad works, Grandpa!"

"Of course it is," quipped Grandpa, not wanting to elaborate.

Grandpa Stu knocked three times on the door. Once at the top, once in the middle, and once on the bottom. The front door swung open by itself. Grandpa hopped inside, pulling Beast and I through. The door immediately slammed shut behind us and locked itself.

On the floor were dozens of ornate rugs. Carpet samples hung from the ceiling like a carpet meat freezer.

"Ah, here it is." Grandpa stomped on one of the rugs in the middle of the room three times. It rolled back revealing a secret staircase underneath it.

"Hurry up, Rudy!"

We stepped down the staircase lit by torches. The rug sealed off the entrance above us.

When we got to the bottom of the staircase, I was somewhat disappointed to find myself in a space not even as big as my bedroom. All around were shelves of books surrounded by an old, rickety table and benches.

Beast sniffed the air and started barking.

"Who's here?" shouted Grandpa. "Show yourself!"

Suddenly, there was a loud SNAP! All the people in the room became visible. There were my parents, Helga, Brett, and most surprisingly, my neighbors—Alan and Barbara Waverly and their son, Bobby.

CHAPTER 23
THE SHELTER

"**Y**ou're safe! Thank heavens you're safe!" said Mom, giving me a big hug, nearly crushing Beast between us. "And you found Beast!"

"That's right. I found him," I said proudly, giving Beast a big kiss on his snout. "With some help from Grandpa Stu."

My dad bounded forward and gave us all one of his famous bear hugs. Beast was barely able to squeeze out before being squashed. "You had us worried sick, Rudy," said Dad, tearing up. "And what are *you* doing here, Pop? You swore you would never leave... that place."

"Things have changed," smirked Grandpa. "But I think the more important question is, how'd all of *you* get down *here*? This is supposed to be a *secret* hideout."

"I brought them here," replied Helga. "They knocked on my door looking for Rudy. It woke me up and this was the only place I think where you might be."

Grandpa Stu flashed Helga a disapproving glance.

"Don't give me that look, Stuart! I feared the worst!" snipped Helga, throwing us our old clothes, which we changed back into happily. Grandpa did a quick count to make sure the potions in his inner pockets were all accounted for. Helga continued, "When I saw that you and Rudy were gone, I thought the bad Ankaras had you and would be coming after us next. I had to bring everyone down here for their safety."

101

"Why them?!" I implored, indicating the Waverlys. "They're bad Ankaras! I saw them with Dr. Yux tonight."

"No, Rudy," said Grandpa, "they're not bad Ankaras. They're moles—good Ankaras who've been tryin' to infiltrate Lyman Yux's order."

"Tonight was the first night Dr. Yux finally invited us to the Ankara's lair," Barbara Waverly said proudly.

Grandpa piped, "Hey Mitzi, show Rudy who you really are," urged Grandpa.

Barbara Waverly snapped her fingers and suddenly the young blonde blue-eyed couple became middle-aged and frumpy. Barbara had black hair with a grey streak down the middle and Alan Waverly didn't have any hair at all!

"These are my friends Mortimer and Mitzi Popplefog," Grandpa said, giving them big hugs. "Mortimer can change himself and his family to look like any kind of person. Mitzi can change herself and her family into any kind of animal with a snap of her fingers."

"Not quite, Stuart," Mrs. Popplefog corrected. "It has to be an animal I've studied and know *everything* about. Like this for instance."

Mrs. Popplefog snapped her fingers again She, Mortimer and Bobby became a family of penguins.

"Why can she only change her family?" I asked Grandpa.

"It's a complicated law of magic, Rudy. I'm sure you can read about it in at least one of these books."

I looked around the room at the shelves of books They seemed to have been hastily stacked on top of one another with no sense of order.

Grandpa continued, "These were all the books we could save about the history and laws of the good Ankaras that Lymey Yux didn't manage to destroy."

Grandpa went on to tell everyone about our miraculous escape from the Ankara's lair. He finished by mentioning that Beast wouldn't be able to "Beast-out" again for at least another week, so we couldn't rely on him to save us again.

Suddenly, I heard my dad shouting behind me, "Abby! Abby, wake up!"

I looked down and saw that my mom had passed out.

"Oh for Pete's sake, Bernie," said Grandpa to my dad, "you never told her about the Ankaras, did you?"

"Of course not!" huffed Dad. "You think a sweet, normal girl like her would marry me if she knew what kind of weirdos we were? I had to keep it all a secret and convince her that I thought you were crazy."

"Well, I guess the cat's outta the bag now. You're gonna have some explainin' to do when she wakes up, sonny. Heh heh."

"And by the way, Pop, why does your secret hideout just happen to be in the basement of my store?"

"Could just be a funny coincidence, but I've seen magic work in mysterious ways."

Beast began licking Mom's face and the penguin Popplefogs slapped her with their flippers. She woke up with a start and seemed immediately disappointed that it wasn't all a dream.

"Who are these people? Why is your father out of the asylum, Bernie? And why are there penguins on me??"

Mrs. Popplefog clapped her flippers and changed her family back to their frumpy selves.

"Honey," said my dad, "there are a few things I've never told you."

"Aw, you can tell 'er later, boy," piped up Grandpa. "We can't stay cooped up down here forever. We gotta form a plan and get outta here. It won't be long till Lymey finds us."

"Everything was going fine until you showed up, Stuart!" Helga bellowed. "Because of you, Yux knows we're back. We've lost the element of surprise."

"Yeah, you're one to talk! You couldn't even protect your own grandson. He's one of Yux's cronies now!"

"How dare you!"

As Helga and Grandpa descended into one of their usual battles, I walked over to Brett. He was sitting on a bench staring blankly at the wall.

"Brett?"

"Yes, Rudy?"

"Are you okay?"

"I'm fine. How are you?"

There was no sign of the Brett I knew. I felt a surge of anger swelling in me. I had to bring him out.

"Why don't you take off that tie, Brett? It makes you look like a geek."

Brett shot back, "Ties make young boys look nice and respectable."

"No. You look like a nerd."

"I look handsome and well-kept."

That was it. I grabbed Brett's collar and tried to forcibly remove his tie. But as I tried to pry apart the knot, I suddenly felt my lungs being crushed, as if a giant python were constricting my body.

I fell on the ground gasping. The excruciating pain disappeared just as quickly as it came.

"It's no use," said Alan Waverly. "The ties are enchanted. We can't even get it off our Bobby."

"A tie makes me look like a million bucks," chirped Bobby.

The Popplefogs rolled their eyes.

I refused to give up. I bounced off the ground, ran over to Brett and slapped him in the face as hard as I could. It hurt my hand... a lot.

I stared at Brett, sure that the smack would snap him out of his trance and he would beat the living daylights out of me. But he just rubbed his cheek where I hit him and said calmly, "Hitting is not allowed. I'm going to have to tell on you."

I slumped over the table. It was hopeless.

Grandpa Stu and Helga collapsed on the benches, taking a breather from their latest fight.

Grandpa Stu walked over to my dad, who had finished explaining things to my mom in the corner.

"Why did you do it, son?" asked Grandpa weakly.

"Why'd I do what?" asked Dad.

"Why'd you come back to Danville? I told you never to come back here."

"Pop, that was years ago. How could I ever explain to my wife that I turned down the job offer of a lifetime and a chance to live in the "best city in the world" because my father in an insane asylum says the mayor is his supernatural arch-nemesis? Besides, the war's been over for so long. No one in the family has any powers, we changed our names. Nobody knew what we looked like, so I thought... I thought..."

"You *weren't* thinking, boy. They found you in Deep Valley and set everything up for ya here so they could get their hands on Rudy. Lymey needs him so that he can implement something he calls *The Great Plan.*"

My mother, finally convinced this was not a dream, piped in, "Rudy? Why do they want Rudy? He's just a normal kid."

"Because," said my dad, "I chose not to become an Ankara. That means if they make Rudy one, he'll have all my powers, plus his own."

"But why not get some other normal kid whose parents aren't Ankaras?" implored Mom.

"That'll do no good," said Grandpa. "First generation Ankaras can't do much more than wiggle their ears or make their nose light up. With each new generation the powers get more and more... well... powerful. The truth is, over one hundred fifty years ago, Rudy's and Yux's ancestors were the very first two Ankaras there was. That means Rudy and Yux are the most powerful Ankaras alive. Rudy could even be more powerful than Yux since his daddy chose not to become an Ankara and he's from the new generation. That's why they're after him."

"They will *not* get my son under any circumstance," Mom declared fiercely. "Bernie, we are moving tonight and getting out of this city. Let's go."

Everyone looked to my dad. He was wiping away tears on his 'Rugs Are My Life' T-shirt.

"You're right, honey. I'm sorry, Pop. All I ever wanted was to keep my family out of your world... out of this war."

"I respect that, son, but you brought them back into it and there's no escaping now."

"No, Pop. We're walking away. We'll change our names again and move to the other side of the world if we have to. Rudy, Abby, let's go. We're leaving."

Dad took us by the hands and led us up the staircase.

106

I looked back at Grandpa Stu, but he had nothing to say. We looked into each other's eyes thinking this would be the last time we'd see one another.

Then we heard it.

The voice of Dr. Lyman Yux.

His hypnotic, soothing words echoed from a loudspeaker.

"We know you're down there. We are your friends. Don't hide from us. Come out and talk to us."

He repeated these words over and over.

Mom once again had that glazed-over look in her eyes like when she listened to Dr. Yux on the radio.

"We should go out and talk to him," Mom said. "He's very nice."

"Dang it!" shouted Grandpa. "Cover her ears! He's casting a spell!"

Brett and Bobby began chanting in unison, "Let us out. Our master calls us. Let us out. Our master calls us."

"Come out from the shelter and no harm will come to you. We see your every move."

He knew where we were! But how?

Everyone ran up the stairs. The rug rolled back and we peered over the floorboards.

The store was surrounded by the entire Danville Police Force and hundreds of evil Ankaras.

The words were repeating: "It's over. There is no escape."

CHAPTER 24
AN OLD GIFT

"**H**mph... there's no way they could have followed us." said Grandpa with hushed rage.

"Well, they obviously did," Helga retorted. "What are we going to do now?"

I gazed out the store window and saw the answer to how they followed us. I'd recognize the tight clothes anywhere. Ms. Covenly.

But she was no longer the perfect creature that fascinated me in class. This was a much different kind of creature.

A She-Wolf.

That certainly explained her curious dietary habits. She must have picked up our scent and led everyone here.

Brett and red-headed Bobby jumped over everyone and ran to the store's front entrance. They banged on the locked door chanting: "Master, we are here. Master, we are here."

We all screamed at them to come back, but they paid no attention to us.

Dr. Yux raised his scepter. A snake of red light slithered through the deadbolt and opened the door for them. Brett and Bobby raced out of the store to the side of their master.

"It's over!" exclaimed Dr. Yux. "Surrender yourselves at once, or I will have to add these innocent children to my *collection*."

"Collection? What does he mean, Grandpa?" I asked.

"Ech, you don't want to know, Rudy."

Helga and the Popplefogs had terrified expressions and seemed to lose their resolve.

"We have to surrender," said Helga, insistently. "I can't let my grandson die that way."

"I agree," said Mom. "We can't escape. We don't have a choice. Right, Bernie?"

"I... I don't know. There might be a way," my dad said.

"What do you mean, son?" inquired Grandpa.

"Remember my favorite birthday present, Pop?"

"The one from your fifth birthday? Of course I do."

"Well... there it is." My dad pointed to an ornate but tattered rug hanging at the back of the store.

"The Magic Carpet!" Grandpa proclaimed joyously. "That'll do just fine. Listen up folks. Here's the plan."

*****

The Popplefogs crawled out from under the floorboards and stood in the middle of the carpet store with their hands in the air as if they were surrendering.

Dr. Yux squinted to see who he was looking at through the Carpet

Diem window. His scepter shined bright red, and his eyes burst wide open. "Great Gossamer! The Popplefogs! My most elusive prey. I finally have you!"

Helga, Grandpa, Mom, Dad, and I all peered over the floorboards, watching intently.

"Be ready!" proclaimed Yux to his order. "They could turn into dragonflies and fly away at any moment. Although, they won't like what will happen to their son if they try something like that this time."

The Popplefogs looked outside and saw Brett and Bobby standing on the left and right side of Dr. Yux. They were surrounded by dozens of menacing Ankaras, eager to use their powers at the first sign of trouble.

The Popplefogs turned around and nodded to us that the plan was moving forward.

They began running towards the front door as fast as their old legs could carry them. They were at top speed by the time they burst through the front entrance.

As soon as they were outside, Mrs. Popplefog snapped her fingers and she and her husband transformed into charging rhinos!

Now, when there's a rhinoceros charging toward you at full speed just thirty feet away, you only have about one second to decide what you're going to do. This time, every Ankara, including Dr. Yux, made the right choice and quickly dove out of the way, avoiding being gored.

All of us still in the basement made a break out of the hole. We ran to the rug hanging at the back of the store. Dad looked at Grandpa with uncertainty as he unhooked the old carpet. It fell to the ground in an explosion of dust. It was about the size of a ping-pong table, just big enough to fit all of us.

Outside, the scene was chaos.

The Popplefog rhinos were making a break for it. The Danville Police, in their blue uniforms and red ties, set up a barricade of police cars, but the rhinos rammed right through them, sending the cars flying like tumbleweeds in a windstorm.

Yux's Battle Ankaras did their best to stop the rhinos with projectiles and energy blasts but they had already made it far into the distance. Their thick rhino skin was like a coat of armor.

"Wait! Where are the children??" yelled Yux.

The Ankaras looked around. Brett and Bobby were gone!

"There they are!" shouted the bulging-eyed Ankara.

And there they were.

Brett and Bobby were each riding on the long nose-horns of the rhinos. Well, maybe not so much riding as going along for the ride, as the Popplefogs had carefully, but in the blink of an eye, scooped up Brett and Bobby by their shirts as they charged past them.

"After them! We can't let the Popplefogs escape again!" ordered Dr. Yux furiously.

Just as planned, the rhinoceros Popplefogs had created the diversion we needed. My parents, Grandpa Stu, Helga, Beast and I all sat down on the magic carpet that Dad had gotten for his fifth birthday over thirty years ago. Dad lightly tapped the back of the dusty rug. It instantly came to life as if it were brand new!

With one mighty slap, off we went, whooshing through the front entrance so fast we had to hold on tight to the fringes to keep from tumbling off.

The evil Ankaras had just gotten back up after the rhino charge when we zoomed over them with the force of a fighter jet, knocking them all down again like bowling pins.

"There *they* go now! Shoot them down!" ordered Dr. Yux.

The Ankaras were confused about whom to target. The cops were frozen, not believing what they were seeing. The police had never actually had to do any "policing" in Danville besides helping old ladies cross the street, since it was "the safest city in the world."

We were gaining altitude but not as quickly as we hoped. All the bodies must have been weighing the carpet down. We could barely get past fifty feet.

Below us, Dr. Yux bared his teeth in anger. His scepter glowed bright red, illuminated the dark scene. He aimed his scepter at us and shot out a screaming beam of red light like a laser.

"Incoming!" shouted Grandpa Stu.

We held onto the carpet with all our might, but the beam came in too hard and too fast. It hit the bottom of the carpet and all of us were knocked off and sent plummeting earthward.

The evil Ankaras grinned and ran beneath us, preparing for our imminent capture as we hurtled toward the ground.

But just as we were about to land in a sea of Ankaras, the magic carpet swooped down and caught us in the nick of time!

"Woohoo! What a catch!" exclaimed Grandpa Stu.

The carpet had a burn hole in its middle. It was moving a little jerkier than before, but it flew off with renewed vigor, sensing the danger of the situation.

Dr. Yux wasn't about to let us go that easy. Once again, he took aim with his scepter and shot a red beam at us, even bigger and faster than before.

We braced ourselves for another rough impact, but this time Helga saw it coming. She leaned over the side of the carpet, and with a mighty yell, shot her own beam of blue energy at the red beam coming toward us.

The beams met in mid-air, creating a fiery, purple explosion at the point of impact, crushing Yux's beam in mid-flight.

"Yeah! That-a-way, sugarlumps!" Grandpa cheered.

For a moment, it looked like we might make it out safely, but then below us, I saw Principal Pooly remove his big black glasses and squint...

Bursts of fire ignited all around us, one after the other. It felt like we were caught in the middle of a fireworks display.

"I'm going to burn you down!" shouted Principal Pooly, "Just like I burned down your house!"

"What do you mean? *I* burned down my house!" I shouted back.

"Ha! With your little toy rocket? You just lit the fuse. I made the inferno."

It was now clear. We'd been set up to move to Danville from the beginning.

The flames continued to burst around us, barely missing the magic carpet. Just when it looked like we might make it through the pyrotechnic hazard, a touch of fire grazed one of the fringes. The magic carpet caught on fire.

My dad tried to pat it out, but it was spreading too fast.

Soon, the entire back of the carpet was on fire. We all rushed to the front. The carpet twisted and whipped itself, trying to extinguish the fire, but the flames just grew bigger, wilder, more fierce.

I clutched Beast tightly to my chest with my left arm while holding on for dear life with my right.

The carpet seemed to be losing its strength. We were drifting downward toward the throng of Ankaras waiting eagerly below us.

"Don't give up, Rudy! Stay with me!" yelled Grandpa Stu.

Mom and Dad held on to each other tightly and moved in front of me, protecting me from the fire, but the flames had consumed almost two thirds of the carpet.

Suddenly, the fire surged forward and the carpet underneath my parents disintegrated.

Grandpa Stu reached out his hand and was able to grasp onto Dad's hand just as he fell. As he gripped Dad with one hand, he held onto Mom with his other hand. Mom and Dad dangled precariously in midair as Grandpa tried with all his strength to pull them back onto the carpet. But they were too heavy.

The carpet was dropping lower and lower until the Ankaras were able to reach Mom's ankles and drag her down toward them. Since we were all holding on to each other, the rest of us were being dragged into the crowd of Ankaras along with her.

Grandpa saw the situation, huffed, and let go of Dad's hand.

My parents fell into the arms of the evil Ankaras.

"Mom! Dad!" I screamed at the top of my lungs.

Below me, I saw the Ankaras pull my parents to the ground and descend upon them like animals pouncing upon a fresh kill. They bound their arms and legs with thick, black chains.

I heard my mother screaming my name.

"Get away from here, Rudy!" Dad managed to shout before a red mist snatched his voice away.

Grandpa Stu, Helga, Beast and I were left on the magic carpet. It was now enveloped in flames and quickly turning to ash. In seconds, the fire would reach us and we would fall into the hands of the enemy.

I shut my eyes and hoped I would wake up in my soft bed. But that didn't happen.

The last bit of carpet dissolved in a puff.

I held Beast tightly against my chest as I plummeted through the air.

CHAPTER 25
THE BEAKS OF EAGLES

In my opinion, there's no question that the coolest movies ever made are the *Lord of the Rings* trilogy.

I think it appealed to me in particular because the Hobbits were small creatures, just like me, but they proved they could have just as much courage, smarts, and usefulness if given the chance.

The one thing that bothered me about the last movie, *Return of the King*, was at the end when the giant eagles came and rescued Sam and Frodo on the hillside of Mount Doom. If these eagles were such good allies, where were they at the beginning of the journey when they could have just flown Sam, Frodo, and Gandalf to Mount Doom, dropped the ring in, and that would be that? It seems like they took a very long and dangerous journey, costing many lives for nothing.

Oh well, maybe the giant eagles were busy building their giant nests and what not.

Unfortunately, I don't know enough about zoology to distinguish between eagles, hawks, and falcons, but when I opened my eyes and saw two giant birds of prey swooping toward me at breakneck speed, all I could say was...

"Look, Beast! The eagles are coming!"

As the eagles swept above me, I saw Bobby in the talons of one of them and Brett in the talons of the other. It was the Popplefogs, changed from rhinos to giant eagles!

Just as I was about to fall into the clutches of the Ankaras, a mighty talon grabbed me by my collar and lifted me skyward. Then the other eagle, with incredible aerial agility, was able to grasp Helga with one talon and Grandpa Stu with its beak.

The Popplefog eagles swooped down and whooshed away so fast that in the blink of an eye we were soaring over the next block. Dr. Yux shot beams from his scepter and Principal Pooly conjured bursts of fire, but the great birds deftly avoided each assault. Moments later, we were flying out of town, straight over the sign that read:

Welcome to Danville. Why Ever Leave?

Marcus, the handsome Ankara with newly bad teeth, took off from the ground and began flying after us. I'm pretty sure that flight was his only power because all he was doing was following us.

The eagle carrying Grandpa Stu in its beak flipped Grandpa onto its back.

Marcus was gaining on us. He was flying straight toward *me!* He must have wanted to wrestle me away and take me back to Dr. Yux.

Grandpa removed a vial of yellow liquid from his pocket. Marcus' hands were inches away from me.

Then, Grandpa's eagle banked downward so that Grandpa was face-to-face with Marcus.

"You fly well," Grandpa said with a smile, "but Superman you ain't." Then Grandpa splashed the yellow liquid into Marcus' face.

Marcus rubbed his eyes and screamed in agony. His face burst out in boils and pus. He dropped from the sky, landing in the treetops of Bellway Forest.

Grandpa let out a sigh of relief. He pulled Beast and I onto the back of the eagle.

117

We flew on for about an hour until we came to the outer rim of the Black Mountains, finding refuge in the mouth of a deep, dark cave.

CHAPTER 26
THE CHOICE

The cave was pitch-dark.

Grandpa Stu took out a bottle of clear liquid from his left breast pocket and tapped on it twice. It glowed like a hundred candles illuminating the cave.

The cave looked like an abandoned campsite. Spiderwebs covered the ceiling like a coat of sticky paint. Dozens of thin cots were stacked against the back wall. The wood remnants of an ancient fire rotted in the middle of the dirt floor. A chalk drawing on the left wall illustrated an intricate map of Danville.

It reminded me a bit of Ice Cream Ivan's cave, only this one was much higher up and not as homey.

"Heh Heh. This old place brings back memories, don't it Helga?" waxed Grandpa.

"Not fond ones," Helga snapped back.

I put Beast down. He immediately scampered around the cave sniffing an array of new smells. Brett and Bobby stood frozen, staring at the orange light like deer caught in headlights. The Popplefog Eagles rustled their feathers before Mrs. Popplefog clicked her talons, changing them back to the frumpy old couple.

"What is this place?" I asked Grandpa.

"It's home tonight. But it used to be the secret lair for us good Ankaras during the War."

"As you can see, your Grandfather spared no expense," snorted Helga.

"Hey! They *never* found it, did they? Unlike your precious Shelter."

Helga snarled at Grandpa, but the Popplefogs jumped in and separated them before anything could start.

"Listen," said Mortimer Popplefog, "it's very late and this has been a rough day for everyone. Why don't we all get some sleep?"

"Sleep?" I exclaimed in disbelief, "Dr. Yux has my parents! We have to rescue them before he..."

"It's all right, Rudy," Grandpa interjected, "Dr. Yux won't be killing your parents. Well, not tonight anyway. That would make no sense unless he wanted to make a lifelong enemy out of you. I'm guessin' he'll be holding them hostage to try and get what he wants. But don't worry, we'll be gettin' 'em back soon enough."

I hung my head and watched as a tear fell, making a small clump in the dirt.

"Try not to worry. You just get yourself some shut eye, 'cause you got a long day tomorrow."

"Tomorrow? What am I doing tomorrow?"

"It's a weekday, Rudy. You got school tomorrow."

*****

I struggled to find that perfect comfort that leads to sleep on the thin cot. I kept feeling things crawling on my legs. I don't think I'd ever felt so tired in my life, but my mind was so worried about my parents and what lay ahead, it wouldn't let my body get any rest.

On top of that, my parents were never exactly the outdoor types, so this was my first time sleeping outside. Heck, this was my first time even sleeping without a pillow.

The small cot was barely better than the ground. I could feel every sharp rock and pebble underneath me. To make matters worse, everyone else seemed to have passed out right away, so I was the only one left awake.

I grunted in frustration, which must have woken up Grandpa in the cot next to me.

"What's a matter, Rudy? Trouble sleepin'?"

"Yeah."

"That's all right. Gives us the chance to talk."

"About what?"

Grandpa stroked his beard, deep in thought for a few moments. "Rudy, have you given any thought about maybe wantin' to hear the Magic Words?"

"I haven't really had time to think about it."

"Of course. Of course. I don't want you to feel rushed, but we don't have time to spare if we're gonna be savin' your mom and dad. You have a choice to make. If you give me the go ahead, I'll whisper the Magic Words to you as soon as you fall asleep. But once I do that, there's no goin' back. You'll be a part of this war whether you want to or not. Maybe for the rest of your life."

"I understand," I said.

"I know you do. But what I haven't told you is that there is another option."

"What?"

"Just as there are the Magic Words, there's also their opposite. The Non-Magic Words."

"Non-Magic Words?"

"Wish there could be a better name for 'em, but we couldn't think of one. The Non-Magic Words do the opposite of the Magic Words. They'll make it so you'll never be able to have magical powers. No matter what. Just like the Magic Words, after I tell you the Non-Magic Words it will leave a mark on you that only Lymey and I can see. I told those words to your father when he was your age and Dr. Yux never bothered him after that. I can whisper these words to you and you can move someplace else and try to live a happy, normal life."

"What do you think I should do, Grandpa?"

"I don't know, Rudy. Part of me wants you to be safe and carefree the rest of your life. But I worry about the world you'll be safe in if there's no one to stop that Lymey Yux."

"And what about my parents? Will we need my powers to rescue them?"

"Seeing as there's no tellin' what powers you're gonna get, I can't say for sure. But we're all gonna be doin' our best to save 'em either way."

I thought as hard as I could. I wish that I could say that I was excited at the thought of getting amazing powers, but at that moment all I really felt was fear.

Two days ago my biggest responsibility was making sure Beast had fresh water and kibble every morning. If I said 'yes' I would be taking on the responsibility of saving not only my family, not only the kids under Yux's control, but maybe even the entire world from Yux's evil designs. And what if Yux got me under his control once I had my powers? I would be more harm to the world than good.

I know all of my friends back in Deep Valley would say 'yes' in a heartbeat, but after today, the idea of living a long, normal life gave me a good deal of comfort. Besides, it's what my parents would want for me, right?

All of this thinking was finally making me drowsy. My eyelids were feeling as heavy as boulders.

The cave became blurry.

Just before my eyes shut, an image passed through my head. I'm forty years old and I'm working side by side with my dad in our carpet store. All of our employees are wearing red ties. Then, I go home one evening and see my children are wearing red ties, their friends are wearing red ties, and even our dog is wearing a red tie...

I whisper, "Tell me the Magic Words, Grandpa."

And fall asleep.

CHAPTER 27
BLUE AND RED

The first beam of the sunrise streamed into the cave, waking me up.

The light didn't seem to bother Beast. He kept right on dozing on his back, his paw twitching back and forth. That meant he was dreaming. I wonder what dogs dream about. When they wake up do they know they were just dreaming or do they think what they dreamed actually happened during the night? If that's the case I hope dogs don't remember their dreams if they ever have nightmares.

But as I was saying, I woke up with the first beam of the sunrise, and the first thing I noticed (after dozing Beast) was that Grandpa Stu was not in the cave.

I looked around and only saw Bobby and Brett, who were still sound asleep.

All the grown ups were gone!

I panicked and started yelling: "Grandpa! Grandpa!"

When nobody answered, it was then that I suddenly remembered.

Did Grandpa tell me the Magic Words?

I didn't feel any different. My body seemed to look the same. Maybe I didn't tell him to tell me the Magic Words. Maybe I fell asleep and just dreamed that I did.

I was very confused and scared.

Brett and Bobby woke up, robotically fixed their clothes so they looked nice and neat, and stacked their cots in the corner.

"Do either of you know where the grown-ups went?" I asked.

"No, Rudy," they answered.

Suddenly a blue flash lit up around them like they were glowing. It disappeared a second later.

"Hmm," I thought. "That was odd."

Then from behind, I heard the unmistakable voice of Grandpa Stu yelping "Yee Haw!" as he and Helga swooped into the cave on the backs of the Popplefog eagles.

Grandpa jumped off his eagle with a big sack on his back.

"Grandpa, where were you?"

"Down in the valley gettin' ingredients for potions we may be needin' today."

The blue glow lit up around Grandpa this time. I rubbed my eyes and the glow was gone. Was it just a trick of the sunlight?

"What will the potions do, Grandpa? What's the plan?"

"There is no plan, Rudy." Suddenly, a *red glow* flashed behind Grandpa and disappeared. "Aw, that ain't true. I can't lie to ya, Rudy. The truth is me and Helga have been working on this plan for a while now. But the less you know, the better."

A blue glow lit up around Grandpa. I think I finally understood. This must be one of my new powers. A blue glow meant someone was telling the truth. A red glow meant they were lying.

Grandpa shuffled to the back of the cave and sat next to a small freshwater spring. He poured out the contents of his sack, forming a big pile of leaves, berries, plants, and bugs. He carefully selected his ingredients and mashed them together between large rocks.

Grandpa, Helga and the Popplefogs were talking quietly. I guess it was about the plan I wasn't privy to. When they were finished I crept over and asked:

"What are you making, Grandpa?"

"I told ya, Rudy, I can't tell you. If things go wrong and they get a hold of you, they'll be doin' terrible things to you if they think you got information."

"Okay. Well, can you at least let me know whether you told me the Magic Words?"

"Rudy, these potions are very hard to do without a blender. I need to concentrate, so hold off for a while."

"Grandpa, I need to know!"

Grandpa huffed, brushing away a moth that had flown into his beard.

"No, I didn't tell you the words. You ain't ready yet."

A bright red flash lit around him.

"Grandpa, I know you're lying."

"Lying? What? Crazy."

"Grandpa, ever since I woke up I've been able to tell when someone is telling the truth or lying. Is that one of my powers?"

"Could be. Heck, how should I know?"

"So you did tell me the Magic Words!"

"Well, if you know when I'm lyin', I guess you already know the answer to that! Makes sense I suppose. You always did have the knack for seein' things as they truly are."

That's right. I was the only who could see when Ms. Covenly was eating the rat in class. This must be one of my powers. But if I have powers, that means...

Oh my gosh! He did it! I was an Ankara! A big smile stretched across my face. Was my life going to suddenly become like the comic books I'd been reading ever since I was eight?

Grandpa sensed my excitement and pulled me close to him. "Don't be gettin' too up on yourself, boy. You were safer before you heard them words. And you're too darn young. I was caught up in the excitement last night. Shoulda slept on it. I'm thinkin' I made a big mistake."

My excitement quickly faded as I came to a harsh realization. How was the ability to tell lies from truth supposed to help me defeat Dr. Yux, the most powerful Ankara on Earth? I thought I was going to get a cool power like Helga's energy blasts or be as strong as Superman. I still had no way to attack someone or defend myself from harm. I angrily questioned Grandpa Stu, "How could this power possibly help me defeat Dr. Yux?"

"Whatever powers you have, you have for a reason to accomplish what you're meant to accomplish. Don't question 'em, Rudy. Just use 'em for good. Now leave me alone."

I turned in a huff and kicked a rock out of the cave.

Grandpa spoke sharply, not looking at me. "And you need to learn to control your temper, boy."

CHAPTER 28
THE THIRD DAY OF SCHOOL

The Popplefog eagles dropped Grandpa, Helga, Brett, Beast and I at the far edge of Danville.

From there they flew back to their home on Cheswick Lane, where they planned to turn back into the Waverlys and take Bobby to school so as not to arouse suspicion.

We walked all the way to Danville Reformatory in silence. I kept waiting for Grandpa to pipe up and let me in on the plan, but he kept his focus forward. Sometimes he muttered to himself under his breath. Even Helga looked nervous.

As the four of us plus Beast rounded the corner at 7:45 a.m., I saw the last thing in the world I expected to see.

"Heh heh! I told ya it would work, Helga!" exclaimed Grandpa, doing a little dance.

From all directions a mass was descending upon the school.

A mass of... old people. *Really* old people.

"Don't worry, Rudy. Me and Helga set this all up. Helga sent out a mailing a couple days ago that said today was *Grandparent's Day* at your school. Heh heh heh! Now we can stay with ya in school all day and they can't do nothin' about it!"

Principal Pooly stood out in front of the school sweating like a pig, greeting all the grandparents as they came in. Judging from his confused look and that of the teachers just arriving, this was a big shock to everyone. They acted like everything was planned, so not to tarnish the perfect image of the school.

Even a photographer from The Danville Dandy was there snapping pictures of the event.

"Grandpa, what about Beast? What do I do with him?"

"Oh, I almost forgot. Look what I got here."

Grandpa pulled a leash out of his pocket and attached it to Beast's collar. Then, he put on a pair of really big, old man sunglasses.

"We'll just tell everyone he's my seein' eye dog! Heh heh!"

*****

Inside the classroom, it was obvious that there were no plans to take care of the dozens of elderly guests in the classroom. There were no chairs for them so they had to either stand behind their grandchild's desk or sit on top of it in some cases.

The grandparents grumbled and murmured harsh whispers to another.

Bobby was sitting next to me with his grandparents behind him. When they turned and winked at me, I got it. It was the Popplefogs in another clever disguise.

Ms. Covenly came in five minutes late after what must have been an emergency faculty meeting on how to handle the situation. She carried her usual two enormous stacks of papers.

"Good morning, grandparents," Ms. Covenly said. "We'll be going through our usual lesson so you can see exactly what a day in the life of your grandchild is like. There will be no special activities or lectures."

Ms. Covenly set down the stacks of papers, then started sniffing the air curiously. She turned to me and saw Beast lying under my feet.

"Rudy Berkman! What is your dog doing here? Get that mutt out of my classroom immediately!"

I was expecting this reaction from her and knew exactly what to say.

"*My* dog? What makes you think it's *my* dog? This is my Grandpa Stu's seeing eye dog. He's partially blind."

I noticed my whole body light up red for a split second.

"But I'm not totally blind yet!" joked Grandpa. "Any ladies in here partial to the partially blind?"

All the grandparents laughed except for Helga.

Ms. Covenly stared at me with such scorn, I thought she would turn into a she-wolf and bite my head off right there. I think she was too afraid of Beast "beasting-out" again.

Her scowl turned into a warm smile. She said sweetly, "Okay then. Welcome Mr. Berkman... and your *adorable* dog."

She was no good at all. How would she know Grandpa Stu was Mr. Berkman and not my mom's father, Grandpa O'Malley? I didn't say anything though.

"Hold on a second!" said Marla Stanley's grandfather. "I thought I was coming here to tell the kids stories about the Depression."

Ms. Covenly rolled her eyes. "If I let *you* tell a story then I have to let everyone here tell a story and we'll get nothing done today."

"You know when we got things done?" exclaimed Vanessa Nesbit's grandfather. "World War Two. I was in the famous infantry unit that—

"NO STORIES, I SAID!" Ms. Covenly bellowed, stomping her foot.

The grandparents gasped, but kept their mouths shut after that.

Ms. Covenly blazed through the morning math lesson on fractions. The grandparents watched with great satisfaction as their robotic children took diligent notes and raised their hands with the correct answer whenever Ms. Covenly asked a question. It made me sick whenever they commented about how cute the kids looked in their suits and ties.

I was still the odd duck out and had no idea what Ms. Covenly was talking about. I took wild guesses whenever she called on me. I got nothing right.

Grandpa patted me on the back and said "good try" after each of my wrong answers. The other grandparents were careful not to look at us, but it was clear that all of them were wondering what business I had being at this school.

Even Brett was a changed student. He didn't miss one question on the blackboard.

For the third day in a row, the lunch bell couldn't have come any sooner.

CHAPTER 29
THE MARCH

"Just one thing before you go to lunch..." Ms. Covenly announced matter-of-factly. "Today will be your first day of Physical Education. You will all go straight to the gym after lunch instead of coming back to the classroom."

I looked at Ms. Covenly and raised my eyebrow suspiciously. I found it very strange that in my previous two days I hadn't so much as seen a gymnasium on campus.

Ms. Covenly smiled back fiendishly, her fangs peeking from behind her lips ever so slightly. "Don't worry, Rudy. You're going to have a lot of fun in gym class."

She glowed bright red.

*****

Extra lunch tables were set up hastily to accommodate the grandparents.

For the first time, real-looking food was served, which I was still very afraid to eat.

Grandpa, Helga, Brett and I sat down at a corner table. No one sat with us. The Popplefog/Waverlys sat cleverly at the table across from ours.

I looked over Grandpa Stu's shoulder to the back of the cafeteria and saw Principal Pooly, Ms. Covenly, and several other teachers eyeing us in case we tried something funny.

Grandpa just sat there oblivious, happily gobbling his plate of chili, creamed corn, and fish sandwiches.

I scraped the food off my plate and onto the floor for Beast.

Taking a bite of his sandwich, Grandpa remarked, "Hey Rudy, you know what you call witches who live at the beach?"

I had heard this one before. "Yes, Grandpa. Sand Witches."

"That's right! Heh heh! I think of that one every time I eat a sandwich."

"And it never gets old," said Helga dryly.

"Unlike you," quipped Grandpa.

Helga was about to stab Grandpa with her plastic spork, but I cut in quickly, which I was very used to doing by now.

"Guys! Why are we just sitting here? When are we going to rescue my parents? And how?"

"Don't know," said Grandpa. "Why? You got a plan?"

He was telling the truth.

"Don't know?! What do you mean *don't know*?"

Suddenly, a loud whistle rang out.

We turned our attention to the front of the cafeteria. A large man was standing in painfully short red shorts and a tight white T-shirt that was almost bursting at the seams.

133

The whistle dropped from his mouth and dangled around his neck. He bellowed like a drill sergeant: "Sixth grade! I am your gym instructor, Mr. Barkly! Line up and follow me to the gym!"

Mr. Barkly began marching in rhythm straight out the door. The class ran up behind him and began marching in a perfect single-file formation.

All the grandparents remarked how cute the marching was. I straggled at the back of the line and followed, but refused to march.

*****

Ten minutes had passed and we were still marching. Up and over hills. Through twisting pathways. Across the banks of Shallow Creek.

All the way, Mr. Barkly was leading the class in chants like:

Mr. Barkly: "Danville is the greatest town!"

Class: "Danville is the greatest town!"

Mr. Barkly: "No one cries and no one frowns."

Class: "No one cries and no one frowns."

And...

Mr. Barkly: "Dr. Yux is one great mayor!"

Class: "Dr. Yux is one great mayor!"

Mr. Barkly: "All his laws are just and fair."

Class: "All his laws are just and fair."

Beast kept trying to run off after a bird or gopher he would spot, but Grandpa held on tightly to his leash, keeping him in line.

We followed Shallow Creek until it emptied into a large cave. Mr. Barkly led the marching students inside the ominous cavern.

"Don't worry, Grandparents," Mr. Barkly shouted assuringly, "the gymnasium is right through here."

I looked at Grandpa with trepidation. The cave didn't look like a place I would ever want to go into. It felt like a trap.

"Don't worry, Rudy. I'm right behind you."

We stepped through the cave, but to my surprise, it was really more of a long archway. It led out to a large, sunny, beautiful grass field.

Mr. Barkly turned to the crowd and announced with pride, "Ladies and Gentlemen, I am pleased to demonstrate the newest in gym technology that can only be found right here at Danville Reformatory and in Tokyo, Japan. *The Retractable Gymasium!*

Mr. Barkly pulled on a lever sticking out of the ground. The grass field began sliding open like a large, mechanical sun roof. The sound of gears cranking and churning was almost deafening. From the enormous opening in the ground, a mighty gymnasium arose with shimmering magnificence.

"In the event of a tornado," Mr. Barkly continued, "we can put all of your grandchildren into the gymnasium, send it underground, and safely wait out the storm."

The crowd applauded and cheered, beyond impressed.

"But that's nothing. Wait till you see the inside!" Mr. Barkly proclaimed.

Mr. Barkly unlocked the gymnasium door. My class and all the grandparents shuffled inside with excitement.

Grandpa, Beast, and I were the last to enter, but before we could, Mr.

Barkly slammed the door shut on us.

"At ease. It will be just a moment for *you* three."

"Hey! What's going on here?" exclaimed Grandpa. "You can't keep my boy from going to his gym class."

"I'm sorry, sir. I'm afraid that gym class has been postponed while the gymnasium undergoes renovations."

"Renovations? What are you talking about?"

With the incredible spectacle of the gymnasium, I hadn't taken notice that Mr. Barkly had been flashing *red* the entire time.

Mr. Barkly smiled, then blew on his whistle in three quick bursts.

I watched with horror as the gymnasium transformed into a menacing gothic tower. In an instant, before me was a dark, ghastly castle made of heavy black bricks and buckled iron.

Shrieks echoed from inside.

"Welcome to the home of Dr. Lyman Yux," Mr. Barkly stated politely opening the door. "Please enter."

Everything inside of me was telling me to turn around and run away. But then I heard a cry from inside.

"Rudy! Please help us!"

It was my mother.

CHAPTER 30
THE GRUESOME COLLECTION

"**R**udy, wait!"

I ignored Grandpa's plea and ran headlong into the dark castle.

I ran into my darkest nightmare.

The darkness outside the castle was nothing compared to the darkness within, though it wasn't a pitch-black darkness. The hall festered with the kind of darkness that only lives in a place of ancient evil. Where evil thoughts and evil deeds crawl up and consume the walls like a sickening ivy. Where the smell reeks like the den of a million spiders that revel in the stench of the countless carcasses strewn below their sticky webs.

Why did I feel so much like a helpless insect at that moment?

Temporary bleachers were stacked all the way up to the ceiling like seats at a football stadium.

Filling the seats were every kid from Danville Reformatory — a fearsome uniformity of gray jackets and red ties, all silently staring at me. My gym class must have taken the long way here to give the other kids time to arrive ahead of us.

In front of the kids was every faculty member, smiling with confidence, dressed in black suits and capes with a single red stripe painted across their chests that made them look like grinning black widows.

The grandparents who marched with us were trapped in a large cage, suspended twenty feet in the air, hanging by an iron chain. All of them were unconscious.

At the base of the rafters was a large platform. On top of the platform was a monstrous throne.

Standing to the right of the throne were my parents. They were wearing gray suits with red ties. Yux had them under his control. He must have made my mom call to me.

Standing to the left of the throne were Helga and Brett. Helga had her hands bound behind her back and her feet tied to the floor by a serpent of red energy.

Standing in front of the throne was Dr. Yux. His scepter, gripped in his right hand and planted on the floor, illuminated the hall with its frightening red light.

The red energy even radiated from the walls, as if it were the mortar holding the ancient stones in place.

Grandpa and Beast ran in behind me.

Dr. Yux extended his scepter and shot a red beam. The beam whirred past my head and split into two lassos. The lassos ensnared Grandpa and Beast. Dr. Yux lifted them into the air.

"Let me go, Lymey! Or you'll be sorry!"

Dr. Yux chuckled as he lowered Grandpa and Beast into a cage that sprang up from the platform. The bars of the cage were pulsing beams of the same red energy that quickly sealed around them.

I stood alone.

"Rudy Berkman, my dear boy, I'm so glad we finally have this chance to have a rational conversation." Yux spoke with authority so the whole hall could hear him.

"What have you done to my parents? Let them go!" I shouted, threateningly.

"Oh, I would Rudy, but I'm afraid they wouldn't go anywhere. You see, they are with me now and quite happy about it."

"Join Dr. Yux, Rudy," my parents said in a monotone.

"See?" said Dr. Yux. "Be a good boy and obey your parents."

"Don't listen to 'em, Rudy! He's a trickster, he is!" shouted Grandpa.

Yux shot a glare at Grandpa, then snapped his fingers. Grandpa's own beard stuffed itself into his mouth so that his voice was completely muffled.

Yux continued, "That's much better. Now Rudy, I hope you're smart enough to realize the situation you're in."

I was shaking and sweating. I tried not to appear afraid. My eyes darted around the room looking for a way out. There was none.

"You and your Grandfather must have thought you were pretty clever orchestrating this Grandparents' Day fiasco. Did you really think you could outsmart me? *Me?* The smartest Ankara alive? How does it feel knowing that your whole plan has backfired? That your misplaced bravery may have only cost the lives of more innocent people?"

My parents stared at me with vacant, loveless eyes. Grandpa, Beast, and Helga struggled in vain to free themselves. At that moment, I honestly felt only one thing.

"I'm confused," I said.

"Confused?" Yux replied curiously.

"Why am I here? What do you want from me?"

"Ah, finally. The big question."

Yux opened his mouth like he was about to continue, then hesitated. He began to walk down the steps of the platform toward me. I stepped back but Dr. Yux stopped, turning toward a coat rack standing in front of the platform. Hanging on the rack was a single red tie.

"I can see that you have the Mark of the Magic Words, Rudy."

A blue flash glimmered around him. He was telling the truth.

"Have you discovered your powers yet?"

"No," I said. A small red glow flashed around me. It was a half-truth since I had only discovered one of my powers so far.

"What a pity," Yux said. "The good news is that under my tutelage, you will not only discover your own powers, you will learn the secret of acquiring unlimited power, you will—

"Shut your ugly mouth!" I interjected, almost not believing I said it.

Yux bared his teeth in rage, shocked that I had the audacity to interrupt him mid-sentence.

"Don't bother with your speeches," I barked. "If you want an apprentice, you can find some other kid. I'll *never* put one of your ties on. I will *never* let you control me."

"My dear boy, you have misunderstood me. I do not intend to *control* you. I intend to *become* you."

"Become me? What's that supposed to mean?"

"I have a plan, Rudy. A truly wonderful plan for things. Every city in the world will be just like Danville – clean, safe, smart, and happy.

The plan is already well under way. Graduates of Danville and my many followers hold countless public offices and run the largest corporations. All of them are taking orders from *me*. But the fact is that I am old, Rudy. And for all my great powers, the one thing I cannot do is avoid the end of my own life, which I feel creeping closer every day. To ensure that my plan is completed and to see it come to fruition, I need to become young again. Rudy, I need to transfer my spirit into your body."

He was telling the truth.

"But why *my* body? There are a thousand other kids in Danville."

"I think you know the answer to that. You are special, Rudy. Your father choosing not to hear the Magic Words did more for you than give you two kinds of powers. You also have the ability to acquire many new powers – as many as you want – but only through a secret means which I was the first to discover. If I am to maintain my power and continue to improve the world, I must remain the most powerful Ankara alive, and I can only do that through you, Rudy."

"Suppose I go along with this. What will happen to my spirit once you take over my body?"

"That's the good news. I will put your spirit into anyone you choose. Would you like to be a baseball player?"

There was a tremendous red flash around him.

"You're lying!" I retorted, angrily.

Yux was taken aback. He wondered what had given him away. He then smiled his fake smile and said, "Very good, Rudy. The truth is... I don't know what will happen to your spirit. This magic has never been done before. Your spirit could remain trapped in your own body, or... you could die."

This was true.

"You're telling me I'm just supposed to agree to let you do this? Why

141

should I?"

"Because Rudy, if you look around, you will see that you have no choice. Just like all of your classmates who have willingly submitted themselves to my control, you must willingly put on this special tie that will allow my spirit access to your body. But if you refuse to willingly put on this tie, then I am afraid that you will die. Your parents will die. Your grandfather will die. Helga will die. Brett will die. And your darling dog will most definitely die. Oh, and I mustn't forget the Popplefogs."

The Ankaras in front pushed forth the Popplefogs, bound and gagged in their true forms.

"Yes, my suspicions about the Waverlys were confirmed when they were the only Ankaras not present that night outside your father's carpet store. They also shall die."

Here I was. Eleven years old, being asked to sacrifice my own life to save the lives of everyone in the world I loved. Three days ago my biggest dilemma was trying to decide between Rice Krispies and Corn Flakes in the morning.

I needed more time. There must be a way out of this. I decided to try calling his bluff, just to buy myself another minute.

"You can't fool me, Dr. Yux. You would never kill anyone. You don't have the guts. Not in front of all these witnesses."

Dr. Yux scowled with such anger, steam was rising from his scary eyebrows.

"Young man, you have no idea what I am capable of."

At that, Dr. Yux waved his scepter forcefully. Gigantic curtains drew back along the towering walls.

On shelves stacked fifty feet high and a hundred feet long, were rows and rows of shining, silver...

Skulls.

Beneath each silver skull was a name, plated in gold. There must have been at least five thousand of them. I was so frightened, I almost fell backwards onto the ground.

Despite their mouths being muffled, I could hear unbridled wails of grief from Grandpa, Helga, and the Popplefogs.

This was truly the most horrible sight I could ever imagine.

"Do you like my collection, Rudy? Each skull is an Ankara that I killed during the War of the Ankaras. To preserve my trophies, I gilded them in pure silver and gave each a place on my shelf. But do you know what the most remarkable thing is? I discovered that each time I killed an Ankara, their powers became *mine*. Yes, Rudy, that is our secret. Whenever you or I kill an Ankara, the powers he or she possesses are transferred to us. I am by far the most powerful Ankara alive. Whatever two powers you possess are no match for my thousands. So let's not waste any more time. Bind yourself with this red tie, and I will free your parents, your grandfather, and all the rest of your friends, including your precious pooch."

He wasn't lying.

Well, I guess this was a small victory. If I refused, all of us would die, including me. If the rest were free, maybe they would stop Yux one day.

I looked up at Dr. Yux, but didn't have the will to speak.

I simply nodded my head.

"A wise decision, young man."

Dr. Yux walked toward me and handed me the special red tie.

"As you bind this tie around your neck, Rudy Berkman, you are binding your spirit in service to me. Your spirit's first act of service will be to surrender its physical form for the occupancy of *my* spirit."

143

I dropped the tie around my neck.

Grandpa, Helga, and the Popplefogs thrashed their bodies but could not come to my rescue this time.

I took a deep breath, shut my eyes. I murmured "Goodbye..."

And cinched the knot upwards.

CHAPTER 31
THE NOOSE TIGHTENS

Sometimes when I'm dreaming, I'll be talking to someone, and the next second I'll be floating high in the air, watching myself talking to the person from above.

Don't ever let anyone tell you dreams can't come true.

No sooner did I feel the pinch of the knot around my neck than I was looking down on the hall from a bird's-eye view.

I saw the body of Dr. Yux fall to the floor. I saw my eyes open. I saw my previous body look curiously at my hands. I saw my body walk up the steps of the platform and grasp Dr. Yux's scepter.

As soon as I grasped the scepter, my eyebrows grew out to the scary length of Dr. Yux's. I saw myself proclaim: "It worked!"

The crowd of Ankaras burst into thunderous applause.

Although I could see all this happening, I could not see any part of my current form. It was as if I was just a floating consciousness.

I saw myself step onto the platform and begin to address the Ankaras with a voice that was deep and unfamiliar.

"My order of Ankaras, just as I predicted, the next phase of the Great Plan is now ready to move forward. With the elimination of our enemies, there will be nothing to stop us!"

I couldn't believe there was nothing I could do. Dr. Yux was going to take over the world using my body and no one was going to stop him.

Yux continued, "And now, my old friends, Stuart, Helga, Mortimer and Mitzi... it is time to finally put an end to your hopeless resistance."

Using my arm, Yux extended his scepter and shot a red beam at the Popplefogs. The beam turned into a noose as it traveled toward them, wrapping tightly around their necks. Yux was strangling the Popplefogs to death.

I was about to be made into a murderer.

A brilliant tunnel of white light opened above me. It started sucking me in. I was waiting for a feeling of acceptance to rush through me, but it never came.

That's when I heard it. Just like when my house was burning down and I was blinded by smoke...

Beast was barking.

Don't ask me to explain how I knew, but at that moment I could understand exactly what Beast was saying with his barks.

"Do not take him!" Beast shouted. "There is still hope. Take me!"

The world became dark. Moments later, I opened my eyes and everything changed.

CHAPTER 32
THE BEAST WITHIN

I was inside of the cage, very close to the ground. I looked up and saw Grandpa Stu struggling to free himself. He was watching the Popplefogs slowly suffocating just ten feet away from him.

I could smell everything in the whole hall. Holy moly.

"I'm Beast!!" I shouted. But all that came out was a loud bark.

Grandpa Stu wouldn't look at me, so I lunged at him in my new beagle body and bit him on the ankle.

Grandpa's cry of "Owww!" was muffled by his beard still stuffed in his mouth.

He looked down at me, and his eyes widened. He was trying to say something but couldn't.

I jumped up and grabbed his beard in my jaws. His beard rolled out of his mouth as I hung from the end of it.

"Rudy! It's you! I see your Mark of the Magic Words on ya!"

I nodded, causing me to swing as I dangled from Grandpa Stu's beard.

"Listen Rudy, there's a potion in my right vest pocket. You have to break the vial open. It's our only hope."

I let go of Grandpa's beard. It immediately rolled itself back into his mouth.

The Popplefogs' faces were turning blue. I only had a few seconds if this was going to work.

Grandpa leaned over so his vest opened up to me. It took three failed attempts before I was finally able to jump up and pull the glass vial out of his pocket with my teeth.

The vial, filled with a green liquid, fell on the floor of the cage but wouldn't break open. I tried biting it, jumping on it, knocking it with my head, but nothing worked.

The Popplefogs fell to their knees, unable to breathe.

I did the only thing I could think to do.

I took the vial in my teeth, then flung it as hard as I could, like I've seen Beast do with his favorite chew toys.

The vial flew between the pulsing bars of the cage, soared over the edge of the platform, dropped a good eight feet onto the floor of the hall, and shattered into pieces.

The Popplefogs fell on their backs, gasping for air that wasn't there.

 148

CHAPTER 33
CRANIUM

Rising like a dense fog from Grandpa's broken vial, a green mist began filling the hall.

Dr. Yux, still in my body, had his back turned, unaware.

The mist snaked upward then split into hundreds of smoky, green arms. The arms of mist drifted to the side walls and onto the shelves that held the five thousand skulls of the dead Ankaras.

The green mist weaved its way across each row, filling each silver skull with its mystical essence. One by one, the skulls' eyes began glowing *bright green*.

Dr. Yux noticed a wave of green light sweep across the audience.

He turned around... and screamed.

Thousands of silver skulls with glowing green eyes flew through the air straight toward him shrieking, "*Murderer!*"

Yux turned his scepter away from the Popplefogs, disconnecting the energy beam that was choking them.

He quickly formed an energy shield around himself. The Popplefogs sucked in air loudly, freed in the nick of time.

The attacking skulls hurled toward Yux, bouncing off his energy shield like rocks skipping across water.

A part of me was glad, not wanting my body to be torn apart.

All five thousand skulls were soaring through the hall, their silver teeth snapping fiercely, creating a frightening sound like a thousand swords and knives clashing together.

The kids of Danville Reformatory seemed hypnotized by the sight. The faculty of Ankaras huddled together, shaking with fear. Some tried to shoot the skulls with fire and energy blasts but the skulls were flying too quickly to be hit.

Even I was so gripped by the fantastic sight that Grandpa Stu had to kick me to get my attention. Again I jumped up and pulled the beard out of his mouth.

"My friends!" Grandpa shouted.

The skulls halted in mid-air and turned their attention to Grandpa.

"Remove the children's ties! They must be rid of them!"

The skulls nodded with understanding and swooped down toward the rafters where the hundreds of kids were standing in their gray suits and red ties.

The frightened children had nowhere to run as the skulls, unable to feel the constrictive pain caused by undoing the ties, chomped off all the children's ties with their sharp silver teeth.

The faculty of Ankaras ran up the rafters, trying to pull the skulls away from the kids.

"Don't forget that one!" yelled Grandpa pointing to Brett.

Several skulls flew toward Brett. He tried to bat them away, but in seconds his tie was torn to shreds and slipped off his neck.

150

The rebellious glimmer immediately returned to Brett's eyes.

The first thing Brett saw was Yux, who he thought was me, using all his power to hold up the force field around himself.

"Berkman! What the heck are you doing?" Brett bellowed.

I was still in the cage dangling from Grandpa's beard with all the strength of Beast's jaws.

"Brett, that's not Rudy!" Grandpa shouted. "That's Lymcy Yux in Rudy's body! You've got to break his scepter!"

Brett walked toward Yux, who was still enveloped in his force field.

"Stay away from me!" warned Yux. "If you touch the force-field, your hand will be burned to ashes."

Brett looked down at his hands and got a strange expression on his face.

His hands started vibrating, then transformed into two shining axe blades.

Grandpa must have whispered the Magic Words to Brett, too!

I couldn't hold on any longer. I dropped to the floor, pulling out some of Grandpa's beard with me.

Brett looked over at Grandpa Stu for instructions, but his beard was stuffed back in his mouth.

"Do it Brett!" yelled Helga.

Brett nodded, took a step forward, raised his right arm in the air, and with all his might, brought it down onto Yux's force-field.

151

Sparks flew like a fireworks explosion, and Yux's force-field broke open like a cracked egg.

Yux stood there in shock as Brett marched inside. Brett turned his right axe back into a hand and the boy famously known as "Iron Fist" decked Yux right in the face. Yux fell over with a broken, bleeding nose. Brett triumphantly snatched Yux's scepter out his hands and held it aloft for the whole hall to see.

"Break it!" Helga urged.

"Nooo!" yelled Yux.

Brett nodded to his grandmother, raised the scepter over his head with both arms, then brought it down forcefully over his knee, snapping it in half.

Yux let out a primal scream of anger as beams of red energy spewed out chaotically from the shards of the scepter.

The scepter must have been feeding all of the red energy in the hall, for at once, the cage that was made of red energy disappeared. All who were bound by the ropes of red energy were immediately freed. Grandpa spit his beard out of his mouth.

Dr. Yux was sprawled on the floor. Bleeding, weakened, vulnerable.

"Kill him now! This is our chance!" urged Helga.

Brett turned his right hand into an axe blade, raised it in the air, and was about it bring it down right onto Yux's neck—my own neck. When he was suddenly tackled from behind.

"No! Don't kill my son!" My mom pleaded, pinning Brett to the ground. Both hers and my dad's ties were chewed off.

"He's not your Rudy! He's Lymey Yux now!" shouted Grandpa.

"I don't care!" Mom cried.

Then my mom ran up to Yux and started wiping the blood off of his face.

Yux sat up and hugged my mom, then looked over her shoulder and smiled.

"Kill them all!" Yux commanded.

Hundreds of evil Ankaras were standing behind us holding dead silver skulls in their arms.

CHAPTER 34
NO WAY OUT

The spell of the skulls had worn off. Their glowing green eyes had fizzled out. There was nothing left to protect us.

The walls and ceiling began shaking. Without the red energy holding it together, pieces of the structure fell all around us like hail. The fortress was crumbling.

There was only one thing we could do. We ran.

Still in Beast's body, I jumped into Grandpa's arms. He sprinted across the platform, leaped off it with amazing agility, and made his way to the door where we had entered.

Fragments of stone the size of basketballs landed in front of us. Grandpa Stu dove out of the way of one, but when I looked up, I saw a boulder-sized rock falling straight toward us. There wasn't time to roll out of the way, but once again Brett was there. He pushed us out of the way at the last moment, saving my life a second time.

"Thanks," I barked.

Grandpa gathered himself and said, "Rudy and me say thanks, Brett."

We were about to make it outside when Ms. Covenly, in the form of a she-wolf, jumped in front of us, drool oozing from her fangs and growling ferociously.

I barked as loud as I could, but that didn't seem to scare her.

Grandpa took a swing at her, but she took his fist in her jaws and bit his hand open. Grandpa screamed in pain as blood poured down his arm.

Ms. Covenly reared back and pounced.

But just before her fangs could sink into us, she was tackled by... I almost couldn't believe it... by Dr. Yux?? Dr. Yux, in his old-man form, was ferociously biting and barking at the very confused Ms. Covenly.

Even in a different body I knew that bark. It was Beast. His spirit was in Dr. Yux's old man body!

Ms. Covenly scuttled away with her tail between her legs.

As Beast howled in triumph, I scratched him behind his old man ear.

We were at the door, but there was no handle. We tried pushing it open but it was a dead end. Helga and Brett showed up and tried blasting a hole through it and chopping it, but couldn't so much as make a dent.

The Popplefogs, in the form of gorillas, joined us in the corner of the hall with my parents over their shoulders. They pounded on the door, but it wouldn't budge.

It was no use. We were cornered.

Dr. Yux proclaimed, "Do not be fooled! That's Rudy's mutt in my body! Show no mercy!"

The hundreds of Ankaras had us surrounded. Principal Pooly stepped to the front of the crowd and raised his glasses. Other Ankaras raised their arms and fingers.

I covered my eyes with my paw. This had to be the end.

But it wasn't.

"Get 'em!" I heard from behind the Ankaras. I knew that voice.

It was Bobby's.

All the Ankaras turned around and screamed in horror.

Every free kid of Danville Reformatory was charging toward them at top speed. In a split second, all the Ankaras were tackled to the ground from behind. They were jumped upon and held down by at least ten kids per Ankara.

Marcus, the handsome flying Ankara with his freshly disfigured face, tried to fly away, but a swarm of kids grabbed onto his ankles, pulling him back down into the melee.

"Follow me!" Grandpa shouted.

Without hesitation, we bolted across the hall back toward the platform. Yux, still in my body, was slumped over the edge.

Grandpa grabbed him and shook him. "How do we get out of here, Lymey?"

"You don't."

The voice did not come from my body. We turned and saw Dr. Yux's previous, *elderly* body standing behind us. Yux spun around like a top and vanished in a cloud of smoke.

Then my own eleven-year old body jolted to life and ran on all fours to us. Judging from the way I was wiggling my butt, Beast was much happier to be in my body than that old, scraggly Yux.

"What's happened to Rudy?" my parents cried.

"That ain't Rudy. Rudy's right here in my arms," said Grandpa. "I'll explain later."

156

"We have to find a way out *now*," declared Helga desperately.

Then, a large chunk of the ceiling fell, hitting my mom right on the head. She was out cold.

"Mom! No!" I barked. She was bleeding. We had to find a way out fast and get her help.

Dad and Grandpa Stu picked Mom up and carried her as we painstakingly searched the hall. There wasn't so much as a window or crack anywhere.

At the other end of the hall, the Ankaras were still fighting fiercely with all the school kids following the lead of brave Bobby.

I turned and saw Brett standing frozen by a shelf on the side wall.

"These are my parents' names," Brett said to Helga. "John Looger and Lisa Looger. Did Yux kill them?"

"Yes. That's the truth," said Helga. "But don't you get angry now. We have to find a way out first."

That's when it happened. I didn't *see* the way out. I smelled it.

I barked at Grandpa and pointed my snout toward a large stone hidden behind the rafters.

"Got it, Rudy," said Grandpa. "This way, everyone."

At the other end of the hall, Mr. Barkly had finally opened the doors and all the Ankaras and kids were running outside as the walls continued to crumble. The awakened grandparents followed behind as fast as their old legs could carry them.

We didn't want to follow behind them and risk getting captured.

We ran between the bars of the rafters to the large boulder. The smell

157

was getting more and more distinct. It was the pungent odor of Mrs. Krimbly's cooking. I barked furiously at the gigantic stone.

"It's behind this boulder," said Grandpa.

"That's as big as a truck. How are we going to move it?" my dad said, incredulously.

Just then, there was a loud crack and a mass of ceiling the size of a school bus crashed down in the center of the hall, knocking all of us off our feet.

"Get out of the way," said Helga, crawling forward. And with one blast of blue energy from her hands, the boulder blew into a million pebbles.

Underneath the boulder was a ventilation shaft.

One after the other, we jumped in and slid down a long metal vent. Dad held onto unconscious Mom as tight as he could. Grandpa Stu held on to my furry body. Helga held on to Brett. Mrs. Popplefog held on to Mr. Popplefog. And lastly, Beast, in my young body, jumped in with a gleeful yelp.

Traveling down the shaft felt like the longest waterslide I'd ever been on. At the end, each of us fell out into an hot tub-sized vat of soup, landing with a splash.

We crawled out of the vat of the disgusting liquid. The kitchen seemed to be all clear.

"Over here!" the Popplefogs hollered.

We crawled through an open window and hopped down onto the school lawn.

Everyone collapsed simultaneously in exhaustion. As I rolled on the grass, I realized why Beast enjoyed it so much. The blades felt blissful grazing against my fur, like a hundred fingers giving me a back-scratch.

158

In the distance we could see the dark towers of Yux's lair rising over the treetops. A low rumbling rolled over the hills that shook the ground. Red light streamed and flashed from the high windows of the towers. In a horrifying instant, the mighty castle collapsed into rubble and an explosion of red energy burst over the hilltop like a grand fireworks finale.

Grandpa smiled, patting me on my doggy head. "Heh. Take that Lymey," he murmured.

I looked up at Grandpa and he took out the last potion from his vest. "You're a cute dog, Rudy, but I liked you better before." There was a splash of orange liquid in my face, and the next thing I knew, I was waking up to Beast licking my nose in my cozy, familiar bed.

CHAPTER 35
THE FIRST DAY OF SCHOOL

No, it wasn't all a dream.

For a moment I thought it was and I was very happy, but my hopes were dashed when I saw Grandpa Stu sitting in an easy chair next to my bed.

"Okay, Beast, I'm awake," I said pushing Beast away.

My nose felt swollen. It hurt when Beast licked it.

"Welcome back to the world, sleepyhead," Grandpa said chuckling.

"How long was I asleep?" I asked.

"Two days," said Grandpa.

"That long?"

"Eh, I'd say a normal recovery time after switching bodies as much as you did."

"That's right! What happened? Why aren't I in Beast's body?"

"Your spirits were both itchin' to get back to their regular bodies. All I had to do was give 'em a little nudge."

"Where am I? This isn't my room."

"That's right. We're in Grapewood now. Looks like we'll be hiding here for a while."

"So my parents are okay? Is everyone okay? Where are they?"

"Your parents are asleep in their room. It's only six in the morning. But I'm amazed they didn't wake you up yesterday. You shoulda heard 'em goin' at it. You think me and Helga are bad? Hoo boy."

"What about Helga, Brett, and the Popplefogs?"

"They're fine, but I can't say the same for that school. Word is they're having a heck of a time trying to run the place now that it's filled with normal, crazy kids again. Heh heh. And not but one will do their homework!"

"So all the kids are okay?"

"Yep. Bobby says Lymey reappeared with a new scepter right after we left. He did some spell that got all the kids back in line and made all those old folks forget everything. But was he ever steaming when he saw his castle collapsed. Hoo boy, we did good getting ridda' that place. I think all my friends' spirits will be restin' in peace now."

"Grandpa, can I ask you a question?"

"Sure, Rudy."

"Why did Yux leave my body?"

"Well, I'm guessin' that once his scepter got broke, the only powers he had were your own. Soon as he realized that your powers weren't enough to defeat all of us at that moment, he had to high-tail it back to his other body so he could vanish himself outta there. Heh. You did good, boy."

"Grandpa, what are my other powers? How do I find them?"

Grandpa sighed and rubbed his forehead.

"Rudy, after all this, do you really think what powers you have matters?"

"Well, don't they? If Yux is still out there, how will I defend myself?"

"Hmmf. Don't ever rely on your powers, Rudy. That's the mistake Yux made. He's spent his whole life doin' terrible, terrible things so that he could be the most powerful Ankara alive. And look what happened. A little kid named Rudy with some courage and help from friends and family that loves him was able to defeat the 'most powerful Ankara alive.' Love is the most powerful thing there is, Rudy. As long as someone loves you, you'll always be more powerful than anyone who wants to harm you."

I nodded, scratching Beast behind his ears.

"Listen to me, Rudy. A fool's the only type of person who craves power. As soon as you got a little bit of it, you're just gonna be wantin' more and more and then some more. No matter how much you get, you'll never be satisfied. Look at Lymey. Back in the day, all he wanted was to be head Ankara of his order. When he got that, all he wanted was to be mayor of our city. Now he won't be happy until he's got the whole world under his control. And after that, who knows?"

"I know. I'm sorry Grandpa."

"Nah, I'm sorry to lecture ya. Your powers will be comin' out as soon you start needin' 'em. My point is, you should pray you won't ever be needin' 'em."

"Grandpa..."

"Yes?"

"I'm sorry I called you crazy before."

"Heh..." Grandpa patted me on the head, his eyes filling with tears

162

which he quickly blinked away. He seemed to want to say something but couldn't quite muster the words. Then he lifted up a big satchel and dumped out about half a dozen thick textbooks on my bed.

"Hey, what are these?" I asked, puzzled.

"Rudy, you got a lot of learnin' to do if you're going to be facing Lymey Yux again."

"Learning? About what?"

"Potions, of course! Just cause it's my magical power, it don't mean I can't pass it on to you the old-fashioned way. Heck, I literally wrote the book on potions, so open up to page one and let's start with basic potion chemistry. We got a lot to get done before your regular school starts at 8:00 a.m."

There was a loud knock at my door and a booming voice from outside.

"Hey BERKman! Wake up already! My grandma sent me over here for some kind of lesson."

Great. Who knew becoming a hero would be such hard work?

*****

Just one more thing before this first part of my story comes to an end. If there are any kids out there reading this who are just starting a new school and you're having a tough time, take it from me, things will get better soon enough.

And if you think you're having a really tough time at your new school, please remember what happened to me my first few days at Danville Reformatory.

I think you'll agree things aren't that bad.

*****

Book 2

THE GIRL FROM ANOTHER WORLD

CHAPTER 0
THE SILENT DESERT

Joe Smally had been driving for twelve hours straight. He even skipped dinner on this, the last night of a three-day haul. His stomach grumbled its disapproval.

Joe chugged a thermos of coffee and glanced at the clock. 2:44 a.m.

"I've timed this just right," Joe thought to himself. "I'll be out of the desert by six in the morning, have the pipes delivered to Mr. Morris by eight, and if I hurry, I can keep my promise to see Crissie before she leaves for her first day of school."

Joe fidgeted in his seat. He'd had to go to the bathroom for the last hour, but there was not even time for that if he was going to make it back to Grapewood before Crissie left. He cranked up the volume on the local, staticky rock station to try and keep his mind off his bladder... when he saw something about a quarter mile down the highway glimmering in his headlights.

Could it be a bicyclist? At this hour? In the middle of the Silent Desert?

As the sparkling object approached, Joe slowed down the sixteen-wheeler to get a good look at the phenomenon.

What he saw was the last thing in the world he expected.

A little girl. No more than eleven. She was walking along the side of the road looking almost angelic in a pretty pink dress with sequins that sparkled in his truck's headlights and silky blonde hair that seemed to glow in the moonlight.

Joe rolled down the passenger window and called out to her, "Little girl, what are you doing out here? Where are your parents?"

The little girl paid no attention to Joe and continued walking past the truck.

Joe thought for a moment that maybe he had fallen asleep at the wheel and was dreaming. He blinked hard to wake himself up, but the scene stayed the same. The little girl continued strolling into the distance.

Again, Joe pulled alongside the girl and called out more forcefully, "Little girl!" Joe sounded the bullhorn on the truck, sending an earthshaking honk echoing through the empty desert.

The little girl stopped, turned, and faced Joe. Her blue eyes shone in the moonlight.

"Where are your parents?" Joe inquired again.

"I don't have any parents," the girl replied in an easy, sweet voice, as if she were walking through a candy shop and not the middle of the Silent Desert at almost three o'clock in the morning.

"Well then, what are you doing out here?" asked Joe, also in a very lighthearted tone.

"Walking."

"I can see that. Where to?"

"Danville."

"Geez," thought Joe, "everyone is going there." Joe's wife was trying to get him and Crissie to move there for years. He continued speaking in as nice a voice as possible, thinking he might look scary to the girl with his three-day scraggly beard.

"Little girl, it's not safe for you to be in the desert all alone. There's not so much as a gas station for a hundred miles in every direction. Danville's gotta be at least three hundred miles from here. Even a grown-up isn't safe wandering all alone in the desert for a hundred miles. Why don't you hop in and I'll take you to the next town? We can try to find your parents."

"I'm not supposed to ride with strangers."

Poor girl. The only explanation Joe could think of was that she was either abandoned by her parents or kidnapped and left to die in the desert. Thinking about his own daughter, Joe was determined not to let any more bad things happen to this girl.

"You're right," said Joe, "you shouldn't ride with strangers. I'm not going to force you to come inside the truck, but if you don't, I'm going to ride alongside you all night to make sure nothing happens to you until the police can come pick you up. But I tell you what, if you're ever feeling too tired or too cold, you can sleep up here in the truck. I promise I won't hurt you."

The little girl stood still and thought for a moment. "Three hundred miles to Danville?" she murmured.

"That's right. I can get you as far as Grapewood. That's just fifty miles from Danville. Are your parents in Danville?"

"No. I don't have parents. Danville is where my school is."

"Well I'll be. I think if we hurry, we could get you to school by morning."

The girl smiled for the first time, showing off her mouth filled with braces. Without a second thought, she jumped into the truck and sat in the seat next to Joe.

"All right then, glad you could join me. What's your name? I'm Joe."

"I'm Sophie."

"That's a pretty name, Sophie," Joe complimented, smiling amiably. "I have a daughter named Crissie who's eight. How old are you?"

"I'm in the sixth grade. How old is that?"

"I guess you'd be eleven or twelve then."

"Yes. I am eleven or twelve."

Joe shook his head and began driving down the highway. "Buckle up and try to get some sleep, Sophie. It's a long drive ahead."

"I don't want to sleep. I want to learn to drive."

"Learn to drive?" laughed Joe. "Aren't you a little young to want to drive?"

"Teach me to drive this... what is this?"

"This is a semi, Sophie. A sixteen-wheeler. I have a special license to drive this."

"Can I drive it, please?"

Joe laughed again, harder. "No! You cannot drive this! Driving trucks isn't for little girls. Ha! Ha!"

Sophie was not laughing.

Her expression became stern and focused. For several minutes there was silence as Sophie studied Joe driving the truck, paying close attention to his changing the gears, his foot on the floor pedals, and his hands adjusting the knobs and buttons.

Finally, after an awkward five minutes that seemed like hours, Sophie again spoke.

"Joe, please take me to Danville."

"I would, Sophie, but I have to go to Grapewood. Once we're there, I'm sure we can find someone to take you wherever you want to go."

Sophie turned her face and stared straight ahead for a moment, then, in a movement so fast Joe had no time to react, Sophie grabbed the steering wheel and jerked it quickly to the right.

The truck veered off the highway, tilted over on its right wheels, then came crashing down hard on its side, skidding across the slippery desert sand. The sound of tumbling pipes clanged and clattered in the cargo bed.

The flipped-over truck came to a rest. Joe glared at Sophie, still buckled safely in her seat.

"Are you okay, Sophie? Are you okay?"

"Yes, I'm fine."

"Why'd you do that, Sophie?! Never, ever touch a steering wheel when someone is—

Joe's words were suddenly cut off by Sophie's hand clasped around his neck. He tried to pull her hand away, but her grip was the strongest he'd ever felt. No air was coming.

Sophie continued to squeeze until...

The next thing Joe knew, the sun was rising over the Black Mountains. He was lying on the ground behind a dried bush about a half-mile from the highway.

He searched himself, but he had nothing on him. No wallet. No cell phone. No water. Nothing.

He tried to scream for help, but his vocal cords were torn and useless – not so much as a squeak could eke out.

170

Joe walked toward the highway and came to the same spot as where Sophie had flipped the truck.

The truck was gone.

It was ninety-five miles to the nearest gas station. There was also a promise to keep to an eight-year old girl in Grapewood. So Joe picked himself up and started running down the highway while it was still cool.

His only chance was that someone driving down the highway would pick him up or report him to rescuers, otherwise the searing heat of the Silent Desert would kill him by nightfall.

CHAPTER 1
MORNING CLASS

KABOOM!

With a loud bang that rattled the walls, my work desk exploded. Flying pieces of wood shrapnel cut through the air in all directions. If I hadn't been wearing my safety goggles, I would have been blinded for sure.

"Doggone it, Rudy!" wailed Grandpa Stu. "How many times do I have to tell ya? It's Roach Juice into Worm Acid, not Worm Acid into Roach Juice! That's the third desk this week!"

"Sorry, Grandpa. I can't tell them apart. They both look like 7-Up to me."

"Aw, you gotta see the details, boy. Look, the bubbles in Roach Juice are tiny, like soda bubbles. The bubbles in Worm Acid are big, like... like big bubbles!"

"Oh. Okay."

There was a knock at the back door. Not because it was locked. The rule was there had to be a "safety knock" before anyone entered the Berkman garage these days in case a magical or hazardous gas was emanating that required a gas mask. Actually, I keep forgetting. It is now called the "Peters" garage. My family agreed it would be a smart idea to change our name for safety. So for now, I'm Rudy Peters.

Whimsical World

More books by Derek Taylor Kent

Visit **WhimsicalWorldBooks.com**
and **DerekTaylorKent.com** for fun and games,
bulk purchases, and to get signed and personalized books.

Text copyright © 2020 by Derek Taylor Kent
Illustrations copyright © 2020 by Derek Taylor Kent
All rights reserved.

Library of Congress Cataloging-in-Publication Data
Kent, Derek Taylor
My Homework Ate my Dog / Derek Taylor Kent
Illustrations by Bright Jungle Studios, Cover Illustration by Angela Koneska
184 pages ; 5 x 7,5 in
ISBN: 978-1-949213-10-2

For information on bulk purchases,
please contact Whimsical World sales department at
info@WhimsicalWorldBooks.com

Second Edition—2020 / Designed by Bright Jungle Studios
Printed in China